BREAKING
Seven

J H I E B

ISBN 978-1-0980-1580-0 (paperback)
ISBN 978-1-0980-1582-4 (digital)

Copyright © 2019 by JHieb

All rights reserved. No part of this publication may be reproduced, distributed, or transmitted in any form or by any means, including photocopying, recording, or other electronic or mechanical methods without the prior written permission of the publisher. For permission requests, solicit the publisher via the address below.

Christian Faith Publishing, Inc.
832 Park Avenue
Meadville, PA 16335
www.christianfaithpublishing.com

Scripture taken from the Holy Bible, NEW INTERNATIONAL VERSION®, NIV® Copyright © 1973, 1978, 1984, 2011 by Biblica, Inc.® Used by permission. All rights reserved worldwide.

Printed in the United States of America

All glory and thanks be to God, who planted the seed of this story in my spirit and allowed it to come to fruition. Without him, this couldn't be. A special thanks to my sister Elizabeth Demery and friend Stephen Fonseca for their consistent belief in me, even when I didn't believe in myself.

PROLOGUE

As she walked down the empty streets, she felt the familiar feeling of paranoia washing over her. Empty storefronts seemed threatening, as if they knew what she was after and condemned her for seeking it. She thought to turn back to the comfort of her friends but couldn't stand to be surrounded by them when they were in the typical stupor and she wasn't. So, she pressed on, hoping Kyle D. would be at his usual corner.

She pulled the thin sleeves of her shirt further down her arms, trying to block against the night's harsh winds, jumping at the sound of leaves crumpling under her weight. The wind mocked her, pulling relentlessly at her hair and dragging it across her face. She wanted to walk in the dim glow of the streetlights but didn't want to be seen by anybody before she could see them, so she clung to the shadows. She knew this area was a popular hangout of the homeless and didn't dare get caught by one of the many drunken ones she had come across before.

She was a few blocks away from her destination when she saw him. At first, she thought to run, but if he was a cop, that would give her away. What innocent person starts running for no reason? So, she tucked her head down and continued walking. Paranoia biting at her heels.

DAY 1

He awoke with a start, in an unfamiliar room. His hair plastered to his face by a thin layer of sweat, which covered his body and soaked the cheap sheets beneath him. His mind was racing to remember where he was while his body was wracked by the chilly air. He groaned, rolling on his side searching for a blanket. Slowly, his eyes adjusted to the dim light as memory of the night before began to piece together.

The woman, she was a mess, track marks on her arms, holey leggings, and a low shirt that left little to the imagination. He had almost walked right by her while following the compass. Had he not glanced up when he did, he probably would have walked in circles for an hour.

Her eyes, the deepest green he had ever seen, caught his attention and made him stop in his tracks. Maybe it was the catlike quality they possessed, amplified no doubt by her thick black eyeliner and heavy mascara, that made him think this was the one.

"Excuse me, ma'am," he asked, "you wouldn't happen to know where one might get a cup of coffee in this area, do you?"

"Are you a cop?" was her hesitant response.

"No, not a cop."

"Are you lost?" she inquired, looking anxiously around.

"Well, I guess you could say that. My compass just might be broken." That part might be true. He had never found himself in an area like this before, and she wasn't the typical package.

"You use a compass?" Again, her eyes jerked quickly around him.

"Well, in a manner of speaking, yes. I guess it's like an internal GPS."

"Oh." This time, her nervous looks seemed to be planning an escape, should he move too quickly.

Just like a cat, he thought, pushing his hands into his pocket as a sign he meant no harm. "If there's a place to get coffee around here and you can take me there, I'd be happy to buy you a cup."

"There's no place to get coffee this late, mister," she said, hesitating. But this time, he could see a deeper need prying at her instinct to flee. "There is a bar though. I'd let you buy me a drink, and I'm sure Phil's got some coffee in back, but no funny business. I'm not a whore."

While he couldn't tell if the last part was a lie, he happily agreed and gestured for her to lead the way.

"What's your name?" he asked, as they headed west across the street.

She paused again, unsure of what name to give, then finally responded, "April."

He pondered for a minute, decided he believed that April was in fact her name, before responding. "April, what a lovely name. It speaks of spring and new life. I'm David. Now, April, I can't help but notice that you look a bit cold. Can I give you my jacket?"

"Won't you be cold?"

"Oh no, I've got a thick sweater on underneath. I doubt if I'll even notice. I've been walking for a bit so I'm fine, really." He slid off his jacket with ease, relieved to be rid of its weight, and slowly handed it to her. He chuckled as she maneuvered her arms into it.

"What's so funny?" she asked, eyes glaring.

"I just couldn't help but notice how that jacket could be a tent for you."

"Oh." The fire in her eyes quickly faded.

They walked the next two blocks in silence, his comfortable hers uneasy, until she finally said, "We're here." As they approached Phil's place, so named he assumed, after the patron of which April spoke earlier, he grabbed the handle and swung the door back, motioning for her to go first. She hesitated for a moment before entering.

"Will you order me a Jack and Coke and a shot of tequila? I need to, um, freshen up."

David watched as she walked slowly toward the bathroom, only heading to the bar when she had disappeared behind the door. The environment, although he had never been to this one, brought back an onslaught of memories from his life before. This was the first bar he had entered in over six years. The first since the night he had failed to save her. Realizing he had stopped moving, he continued toward the bar, pushing those memories back into the deepest realms of his mind, and ordered the drinks. A Jack and Coke and shot of tequila for her, and a black coffee for himself. Considering the time, he was not surprised by the lack of customers, and the drinks arrived quickly.

Taking a sip of the watered down, stale coffee he took in the room. Two men with enough teeth between the two of them to fill one healthy mouth, played pool in a corner, cheered on by a woman with equally devastating dental hygiene and a face covered in acne and too much orange makeup. Across the long bar sat a man in his early fifties with a balding head and cheap suit, who looked as though he had recently been kicked in the shin. The man rubbed fiercely at his temple, as though he was trying to push away his own memories.

David waited on the compass to point to the downtrodden man, but it remained steadfast in the direction of the bathroom. He glanced down at his watch, surprised to discover he had been sitting alone for nearly ten minutes. He gazed once more around the room, beginning to wonder if April had snuck out the back. The compass remaining in the direction of the bathroom, along with the two drinks that sat untouched in a puddle of condensation on the bar in front of him, reassured him she had not. Another five minutes passed before she finally arrived at the bar stool beside him. She shook herself out of his jacket and laid it carefully over the back of the chair before taking a seat.

"I thought maybe you'd left," he said, taking a sip of the bitter black coffee.

"I guess I could say the same thing," she responded, throwing back the tequila without a trace of the grimace he had seen on the faces of young women in bars, all those years ago.

He could tell she had attempted to clean up. The thick makeup around her eyes seemed less smudged, and she had folded her hair into a neat braid, falling well past her shoulders. He was surprised by the way she appealed to him and quickly pushed away thoughts of what it might be like to run his fingers through that long dark hair.

"So, what is it you're doing around here, David?" she asked without breaking eye contact with him. Whatever reluctance she had toward him initially seemed to have dissipated in the safety of Phil's.

"That's kind of an interesting question. Can we come back to it?"

Her brows furrowed, and the fire returned to her eyes. "What is this, some sort of ruse? To what, rob me? Well, jokes on you. I don't have anything worth taking and if you're one of those serial (she pronounced it cereal) killers, you're going to have to find someone else. I brought you to this place because Phil, the owner, is my dad's cousin."

Again, he questioned if that last part were true. If it was, she had again surprised him with her catlike nature, a quick thinker with a cunning side. "No, I don't want to rob you, so to speak. Although I am certain you have something worth taking. I never steal, I always ask." He winked. "As for being a serial killer, no I swear. I've never even hit an animal driving."

The fire once again faded, but her look of skepticism did not. "So, you can drive?"

"Yes."

"But you said you've been walking for hours?"

"Yes."

She shook her head frustrated. "Then why are you walking?"

"I enjoy it."

"You enjoy just walking around in areas like this, at night? Most people avoid it down here even during the day."

"Yes."

"Yes what?" She sighed heavily.

"Yes, I enjoy walking in areas other people avoid."

"You're being elusive," she said, waving down Phil for another drink. "What did you mean by your compass was broken?"

"Well, I thought it might be, but I don't think so anymore." He glanced toward the corner at the sudden squeal of the orange-faced lady.

April followed his gaze. "Why did you think so?"

"I couldn't find what I was looking for," he answered, meeting her eyes once again.

"But you did?"

"Yes, I think so."

"At Phil's?"

"I guess you could say that."

"Well, you keep looking at the guys in the corner, are you a bounty hunter?"

He laughed at the accusation, causing the fire to return to her eyes—those brilliant emerald eyes.

"What's so funny?"

"I'm not laughing at you, April. I'm laughing at the idea of myself as a bounty hunter."

"You look like you can take care of yourself."

"I walk, remember?"

"Walking doesn't give you all of *that*." She waved her hand in a circle around his chest and shoulders.

He refrained from laughing at the action, for fear it would make her eyes burn once again. "Well, sometimes, I walk to places that require climbing."

"You walk and you climb, but you aren't a bounty hunter?"

"Yup."

"Then what do you do?" She slurped from her straw attempting to get the last of her drink, glancing up at him with a smudge of pink running across her nose and cheeks, as if embarrassed by the sound produced by the straw.

"I supposed you could say I'm an acquirer."

"Like antiques?"

"Eh, kind of like that I find and take things people don't realize they don't want."

"What does that even mean?"

A terrible wrenching in his stomach brought him suddenly out of the dreamlike memory.

When her eyes fluttered open, she found herself surrounded by sights she hadn't seen in over six years. Framed pictures of her mother and father, light pink paint on the walls, and the sun gleaming off a high school volleyball trophy. Her childhood bedroom. How she got here was not as clear as the memories that drove her away in the first place.

Pushing back the floral quilt, she looked around the room, anxiously searching for her purse and cigarettes. She hadn't spoken with her mother since she moved out. Hadn't even tried, although the first few months, Maye left several hundred voicemails. *How on earth did I get here?* she thought, digging through her purse. *I don't think I scored last night.* Frustrated at the missing pack, she threw her purse down.

"April, are you up?" She heard her mother's voice call from the hall.

Crap, crap, crap. "Uh, yeah. I'm up." She pulled the covers higher, as if to shield herself from whatever an encounter with Maye might produce. The door slowly opened, and her mother entered, looking nearly the same as six years prior, with only a few extra pounds and a little more grey around her temples, as proof that time had passed. "Uh, hi, Mom."

"Oh, honey, I'm so glad you stopped by last night. Such a pleasant surprise to see you, and you just seemed so happy."

"Was I drunk?" April asked, pushing herself closer to the headboard.

"Well, I thought so at first, but you kept going on about some healer you met at the bar."

In a flash, the memories of the night before jerked her forward, her breath catching in her throat.

"Oh, honey, what is it?"

"Mom. He was real! I thought I dreamt him, but I remember now. The man with the compass, David."

"Well, let's go down and have breakfast. You can tell me all about it. I made pancakes, and your cigarettes are on the counter. You told me to throw them away, but I know how you get without them."

"I don't think I'll need those anymore," April said, pushing the sheets down.

He was not prepared for the violence that took over his body. He had an urge, a *need* for something like he had never felt before. He expected, based on the marks he had seen on April's arms the night before, that "something" was heroin.

He had taken a lot over the past several years. From physical pain and fear, to crippling anxiety, but he wasn't prepared to handle the detox associated with her addiction. As he retched into the garbage pail he had placed near the bed, he felt another emotion that was new to him. Shame. He had experienced guilt. In fact, there hasn't been a day in six years that he didn't experience guilt and sadness from her death, but this was unlike anything he had felt before. He felt dirty somehow, worthless and objectified. That was new.

The clock on the bedside table showed 12:01 p.m. He had slept, if you could call it that, for nine hours and was still riddled with exhaustion. He felt somehow empty, another new experience. That partnered with the uncomfortable numbness in his fingers, and the consistent nausea had him understanding why it was so hard for addicts to quit. While he had never experienced this before, it wasn't the first time he had wished he stayed home; lived a normal life with a nine to five. That wasn't in his cards.

He had made a promise all those years ago, and he wouldn't back out of it now. Rinsing the pail in the hotel bathroom, he thought about the night he lost her. "No, not now," he said into the dark room. He didn't have the energy to reminisce or wish for a life that he would never, could never, have.

Exhausted from shivering and vomiting, he fell back into the damp hotel sheets. "We got her, God," he said, surrendering to sleep.

Splashing cold water on her face, April attempted to pull herself out of the dreamlike state she had been in since waking up. She remembered him vividly, he was after all the type of man one didn't forget easily. Learning he was real was almost as shocking as the possibility that she could dream up such a man. Not just the way he looked, but the cool confidence he walked with and his apparent "gift" for taking.

When she had first spotted him on the street, she had thought for sure he was either a cop or some uptown guy looking to score, not that he would fit in on wall street, but at least comfortable hanging with those GQ types. He certainly didn't fit in with her usual crowd, skater-boy wannabes in jeans too tight and shirts too loose on frail undernourished frames. She still wasn't sure exactly what he did for work, although his self-proclaimed title of acquirer seemed fitting.

She thought about what he had asked of her. The way he assured her that he would never take something that she wouldn't willingly give. At first, she thought it might be some sort of weird fifty shades situation, making him laugh, which in turn had infuriated her. His attempt at an explanation didn't do much to clarify either. Her mother's voice calling her name brought her back to the bathroom. The sink nearly filled with water. She quickly shut it off, dried her face and hands, and yelled, "Coming." down the stairs.

As she neared the kitchen, the scent of pancakes and warm maple syrup overpowered her nose, causing her mouth to water and stomach to growl. She wasn't entirely sure when she had last had a full meal, or any real food for that matter. Most days, dollar menu fries and ranch sustained her. Well, that and whiskey.

"How many would you like?" Maye asked.

"I'll start with one. Thank you."

As they settled at the table, her mother looked at her expectantly. "So who is David and what did he take from you."

"I don't even know where to start, Mom. You might think I'm crazy."

His mind was gripped by anxiety, torn in two worlds of reality. In one, she was still alive, laughing, singing, and cracking jokes at his current condition. In the other, she was dead. He tried to cling tightly to the world he was in, gripping onto the metal bedframe. Telling himself that this was real, that this dingy room was his reality. His brain had another plan. His brain demanded the euphoria it had been denied, although it had never actually felt the euphoria it sought.

So, he watched, as a memory of her danced through the room, fluttering around in a whimsical dress, and he wanted whatever it was that made this all so real. He remembered briefly the woman at the bar, the way the scabs were formed on her arms. *She should have been wearing a jacket out that late*, he thought, realizing immediately how ridiculous a thought it was. Suddenly, she was there too. They danced and laughed together, her dark hair loosed from the braid she had tied it into in the bar.

As his mind formed a new reality, one where Hope and April were apparently friends, he felt his stomach retch, fighting to purge. He rolled off the bed, barely missing the end table, and found the garbage pail. His mind dodging from one thought to the next, unable to still, to focus, to sleep. He thought of the song "Amazing Grace" and watched the two ghostlike dancers as he finally found rest on the floor.

After two pancakes, April finally felt full enough to slow down and explain her encounter with David. Maye looked like she might climb out of her own skin with anticipation. Taking a deep breath, she began.

She told about the handsome man on the street, the man who called himself an acquirer, while watching her eagerly sip down the beverages, which had bought her time. She spoke of their conversation, as the sun rose higher in the sky, highlighting the gold flecks in her eyes.

"He offered to take it, Mom. He said God sent him to me, but not like an angel. He said he's just a man, but the Holy Spirit uses him as a vessel to take things."

Maye paused with their dirty plates in hand, a worried look on her face. "Take what, April? This isn't some weird sex thing, is it?"

"Oh no, Mom. Nothing like that." She didn't add that the thought had crossed her mind when he had first explained what he did.

"Then what?"

"My addiction."

Her mother dropped the dishes in the sink, the clinking and clamoring of glass meeting glass, an appropriate soundtrack to the look of confusion on her face.

"I know, Mom, I know. It sounds crazy, but it's true. He said he could take it. I just had to be willing to let it go."

"The weird sex thing is sounding pretty good right now," Maye mumbled. "How long has it been since you used?"

"Yesterday morning."

"So you were high when you met him?"

"Oh god, Mom. Not at all. That's why I was down at Phil's. Kyle is usually there."

"Yeah," Maye exclaimed disgusted, sitting heavily back into the chair. "I wish you'd stay away from him."

"Mom, Phil's like my uncle."

"The man who helped your father leave us is not your uncle."

April's eyes flared, the familiar anger rising. "He didn't leave us, Mom. He left you."

"Oh, here we go again. Blame me, again. Some things don't ever change I guess." Maye stormed to the open window and lit a cigarette.

"Yeah, well, maybe he just got sick of your constant booze and pill hangovers and…" She paused, the smell of smoke lingering around her nose. Maye looking at her expectantly, feet parted as though she was preparing for battle. "Wait. Mom, I don't want a cig."

"So, what's your point?" Her mother fumed, exhausting a plume of smoke from her mouth.

"We've been down here for hours, and I haven't wanted one. Then, we started arguing and I still didn't want one, and now you're smoking, and I smell it, but I still don't want one."

"Come on, April, not wanting to smoke is a far cry from being healed of a heroin addiction."

"I know, I know. I'm sorry I snapped at you. Please just come sit down and let me finish." Begrudgingly, Maye snuffed out her cigarette and returned to her seat. "Okay. Go on."

April continued to recount the previous evening. She told about David's claim to be able to take people's pain, how skeptical she had been, and how he said he had traveled from Kansas, sometimes hitchhiking and sometimes walking, stopping now and again to help people like he was there to help her. She told of his compass, an arrow in his brain that pointed him to certain people. How sometimes the arrow just sent him in a direction, just to move and how sometimes it pointed to a specific person, like her. When she asked why, he responded saying only that he didn't know. That it wasn't his job to decide who to help. His job was to trust God and let the Holy Spirit do the work.

She told about how he had asked if she was willing to give it up and how when she had asked what it was. He responded that he didn't know, that it was hers to give up and if she would give it, he would gladly take it. "Will it hurt?" April had asked.

"Sometimes, it does," he answered honestly, "usually because people have been holding onto it for so long. It becomes like a part of them, and sometimes, giving up a part of yourself hurts."

She went on to tell how she had gone outside to smoke, to think about his offer, and how while she was smoking, watching him through the window, she decided she trusted him. How as if in that moment, David had known her decision, paid the bill and come out. "Are you ready?" he asked. Scared, she nodded yes. "Will you allow me to take it?" She had responded with a shallow yes.

April told about how he pulled her into his arms for a hug and silently whispered words she didn't understand over her. How he then kissed her on the forehead and said, "God bless you. In the name of Jesus, your chains are broken." She told of how he walked away into the night, without another word.

"And then I woke up here. I don't remember coming here, talking to you, or going to sleep."

DAY 2

He hadn't left the floor in nearly twenty-four hours. Whatever pain he thought he was experiencing yesterday was nothing like the death that rattled his bones today. He tried to recite his favorite verses, but his mind was foggy and unfocused. Almost as bad as the physical pain was the violent smell accosting his nose. He knew he needed to shower but didn't trust his ability to make it to the bathroom. At least here, on the floor, he was able to avoid vomiting.

He found himself wondering what it was that would bring such a young woman to a life like this. He couldn't imagine ever wanting to try the stuff, let alone coming back to it after experiencing any version of withdrawal. The length of his withdrawal symptoms told him that she wasn't new to the world of drugs. He was curious about her, intrigued by the fire in her eyes.

Rarely was he pointed toward females. Not necessarily that they didn't need his help, they just tended to want to "deal with it" themselves. Men, on the other hand, were quick to hand it over. Not always but most of the time. In nearly seven years, he had encountered only a handful of women. Typically, they were dealing with some sort of abuse, either physical or emotional, and needed to be severed from their abuser. When he took whatever the pain was from them, they were able to break ties to the aforementioned. At least, that's how he saw it. In all his years of taking, he had only ever kept in touch with one. The one who started it.

His mind began to wander again back to April. What type of woman could she be now? In the fetal position, he stayed on the hotel floor, imagining the life that April might have now that she was freed from her addiction.

She was already exhausted by her newfound freedom. Maybe exhausted was the wrong way to describe it, maybe she was just bored. Any other time she felt bored, she would have a quick fix, but drugs had no appeal to her now.

Maye called into work sick Tuesday and had requested additional time off, which was almost as exhausting as the boredom. Maye wanted to know everything, and April didn't have the time or patience to try to explain it. How do you tell your mom you have slept in cars, on benches, and with random strangers? So, she told the good parts. Good might be a stretch, she told the less bad parts.

Now, on day two back at home, her mother insisted on card games. "Just like when you were a girl." The last thing April wanted to think about was when she was a girl. The reason she left was sitting across the table, laying down a Skip-Bo card.

"So, where have you been staying?" Maye asked, looking over her cards.

"Well, I was staying with Trish, but I have a feeling that's not going to work. She's probably already sold what little I had, that's if she was sober long enough to consider doing so." She thought of the friend she'd been tethered to for the past two years and wondered how long Trish would even remember her name.

"You can stay here as long as you'd like. It'd be nice to have the company. I have *the* best idea. Why don't we go get you some new clothes? I can't imagine you're going to want to dress in my old clothes for long."

"It's okay, Mom, really. I don't mind. I'll find a job or something and will be able to move out of your hair."

"Really, April? You've been home what, less than forty-eight hours and you already want to leave? Why can't you let me do something nice for you? I haven't seen you in nearly a decade."

April sighed, after being away for so long, she had almost forgotten how Maye was able to push you until she got her way. "Mom, it hasn't been a decade. I just don't want to intrude."

"This is your home. I don't understand why it's so easy for you to forget that."

"This was my home, Mom. It hasn't been in a long time."

"That was your choice, April. How about you just give it another chance? I'm not all that bad. Besides, what else do you have going on? You really shouldn't be going back to whatever den you were in. You know how easy it is to fall back into old habits. Just because he took it once, that doesn't mean you're immune to it."

She could feel her mother's doubts about her recent 'healing' from across the table. "Okay, Mom. I'll stay around. We really don't have to go shopping."

"I know we don't have to, but I would really enjoy having a girl's day together. We can get lunch, maybe get our nails done, or see a movie. Wouldn't that be nice?"

"I'm really tired. It's been a strange few days."

"April, can you just try to act like you're happy to be home."

"I am truly happy to be back, Mom. I just, I just need some time to settle in. This is all so strange."

"You're the one going around giving your 'addiction' to strangers."

"I told you, it wasn't like that. I don't actually know exactly what it was like, but I do think he was a good man. Honestly, I think you'd like him. He was very good-looking."

"Well, in that case, you should go find him. Let's get you married off, then I won't have to worry about you."

April rolled her eyes. Ten seconds ago, her mother was begging for a girl's day, and now she was trying to marry her off? "I doubt a man like that would have any interest in me. But I will say, I'm curious about him. How does he even do what he does? It doesn't make sense."

"Don't roll your eyes, you're too old for that. It really doesn't make sense. Why don't you try to find him?"

"How? You think he hangs out at bars? I did dream about him though. Well, not really a dream, it was like a memory. I just dreamt about meeting him again."

"That sounds like a sign. Maybe he's your prince charming. See, we need to go get you some new clothes, so you can meet him looking like a princess, not like a—"

"Thanks, Mom."

He finally stopped vomiting long enough to eat one of the protein packs he had stored in the room's mini fridge. While he was through the worst of it, he was still riddled with muscle aches and, worse still, joint pain. His knuckles were stiff, barely bending when directed to do so by his brain. He had tried to open the little snack pack with his hands but couldn't grip the thin plastic covering and ended up pulling it back with his teeth.

After eating the small amount his body would accept and sipping some Gatorade, he was exhausted again. He hated being trapped in the room. He spent so much time outdoors. This felt more like a tomb than a hotel room. He tried to watch TV, something to slow his mind, but the available channels held nothing of interest. One was running a *Law and Order SVU* marathon, and the other was some sort of housewives' reality show. He turned off the small TV and pulled his phone from the charger. Music always helped, specifically hymns.

After making the bed, he lay back with headphones in his ears. Drifting into a sort of half sleep, he began to dream of her.

She was on the stage a tambourine in one hand, a microphone in the other, singing with the church band. Her blonde hair flowed from her head like a halo, and her smile invited everybody in, made them feel like they were welcomed into her wonderful world.

"Come on, David," she called from the stage. While he was comfortable playing his acoustic in private with her, it took him much longer to warm up to the idea of standing on the stage being watched by all the churchgoers. Granted, it was unlikely anybody would be looking at him. Her voice seemed to invite the angels into the building, and the presence of the Holy Spirit seemed to ride in on her voice like a wave.

Their parents disapproved of this type of worship, preferring the old-style hymns and church chorus over the more modern worship band, which was part of the reason he had avoided joining this church for as long as he did. It almost felt like an affront to the family to attend separate churches on Sunday, of which they reminded him frequently.

"I'll watch for now," he told her as the band continued to practice.

Sleep came easily on the back of the dreamlike memory.

If she thought cards was exhausting, shopping was even more so. Maye took her to the mall and insisted on entering every store, even the random pet store that had little more than mice and lizards. It's not that she didn't appreciate the gesture, she just didn't want to wear a bright pink dress any more than she wanted to poke her own eyes out. Eventually, she figured out that accepting one of Maye's suggested items, allowed her to choose something more her style without causing offense. So, her arms were packed with an eccentric mixture of bright girlish clothes and more muted natural tones in the form of sweaters, jeans, and button up flannels.

"I am starved," Maye exclaimed when they had left a store geared toward clubbing and dancing. "Do you want to eat here, or should we just grab something on the way home?"

"If it's okay, can we just get something fast? I don't know why, but I'm really tired."

"Probably aren't used to being up at this time of day, are you?"

April let the jab roll off. "No, probably not. Not used to waking up at 7:00 a.m. either."

"Sorry about that. I was really excited to spend the day with you. I guess I didn't think about your lack of a schedule."

Tempted to lash out, April held her tongue, asking instead, "When are you going back to work?"

"Friday, I think. I can stay home longer if you'd like. I haven't used any sick days this year, so they are piled up."

"No, that's fine. I should probably start looking for a job."

"Why don't we ask around here before we leave? I bet this would be a great place to work. So many things to do on your break."

"That's a good idea. I'll come back here then." Her introvert side cringed at the thought of spending a lunch break surrounded by the mall people.

Maye talked the whole drive home, not a single word about her own life, mostly just gossip about her friends or coworkers. When they finally got back to the house, Maye unpacked the fast-food bags on the table. "Come, sit. We can chat some more."

Begrudgingly, April complied. Not wanting to cause another debate. With a mouth full of hamburger, she asked, "So, what have you been up to? Doesn't seem like too much has changed around here."

"Not much at all. Still working at the nursing home. It's not a dream, but it's steady and doesn't pay half bad. The house is paid off now, so I don't have to worry about too much."

"Seeing anybody?"

"No, not really. Tried dating for a while, but I just never really felt like having anybody in my life again after your dad."

"Do you ever talk to him?"

"No. Don't think he'd care to either. I'm sure you see him around."

"I did for a while. He spent a lot of time at Phil's back then. I think he was even working there at one point. Eventually though, he quit drinking and moved to Post Falls. He tries to call me every once in a while. I guess I just don't have the energy to disappoint him again."

"I know how that feels."

Stuffing the last bite in her mouth, April excused herself, ready for bed.

She sat at the vanity in her room, slowly brushing out her hair. She thought about him again as she did. What a mysterious thing to do, walk up to someone, take their infliction, and walk away without another word. She desperately wanted to know more about him, about what he did and what it meant for her. She had tried to get clean before but had usually given up about this time. Now, she didn't even feel the slight tug of yearning at the back of her mind. This might actually be it. If it is, that meant that he did actually possess the gift he claimed. No amount of placebo effect could fight the desire for this long.

If it was real, she was almost disappointed. Not at being clean, that was amazing, she just couldn't imagine that her life would change so drastically and yet remain so incredibly dull. Not sure she could handle another night in the house, she was tempted to call Trisha and see if her room was still available. Mom was right though, no good could come from going back there, and just because he'd taken it once, didn't mean he'd be around to take it again. She would like to believe that she would be able to turn it down with this newfound freedom, but every addict thought that and typically, if put back into a situation where people were using, fell prey to the temptation.

Why me? she thought. There had to be better people to "take" from. Her issues were self-inflicted. It's not like a random junkie walked up to her and stuck her with a needle. She could have stopped. *I didn't deserve this.*

She crawled into bed, feeling almost empty. It wasn't much, but junkie was the identity she had lived with for years. Losing that was almost like giving up a friend. Now, she was just some girl living with her mom. *Better than being homeless, I guess.*

DAY 3

He jerked violently from a deathlike sleep, the final waves of nausea subsiding like the afternoon tide. He laid still in the darkness, waiting for another wave to hit. Eventually, he felt sure that it had passed, so he reached to the nightstand for his phone, the bright light from the screen burning his eyes when he tapped the Home button. Blinking rapidly, he waited for his vision to clear before searching for the date, Thursday, two days since he met her. Unsure of what to expect, David had paid the front desk for ten days, which was apparently considered long term for the place, which boasted nightly and hourly rates.

After his first cross-country trip, he had learned the value in planning ahead. There's nothing quite like enjoying some unknown physical or emotional pain and not having the mental capacity to get to or pay for lodging. One night, sleeping on a park bench in Rapid City had taught that lesson. Since that one unfortunate encounter with local authorities, he now found a hotel, more aptly called a motel, when he first arrived in an unknown city.

Oftentimes, friends or churches would offer him a place to stay, but he could never be sure of who he might meet or what affliction he might take on. So, it was shady motels with dirty carpets and sheets that could pass for potato sacks. Normally, he wouldn't pay for such a long stay, but something in his spirit told him this one would be different. Not that any two had been alike, but generally after dealing with something, whether it be depression or some physical condition, once was enough to give you an idea of how you would handle it the next time. This time, there was some voice in his head telling him it would be longer.

He never minded these extended stays. Typically, he enjoyed them. Since leaving Kansas City the first time, he had seen more of the country than most. Both big cities and towns so small they didn't have a post office. He had helped people like April, and he was happy to meet them, speak to them, take from them, and move on to the next. This one though, this one was different.

His body ached with a mix of fatigue and hunger, along with the unexpected desire for a cigarette. *Well, that's new*, he thought, filling a plastic cup with water from the bathroom sink. He climbed back on the bed then checked the nightstand for a Bible. He had an app on his phone, but always preferred the feel of pages in his hand and the smell of worn paper in his nose. Finding the barely used black book, he opened to the book of Psalm 25. He read out loud.

"O Lord, I give my life to you. I trust in you, my God. Do not let me be disgraced or let my enemies rejoice in my defeat. No one who trusts in you will ever be disgraced, but disgrace comes to those who try to deceive others. Show me the right path O' Lord, point out the road for me to follow. Lead me by your truth and teach me, for you are God who saves me. All day long I put my hope in you. Amen."

He hadn't prayed his own words since Hope's death. Partly due to fear of what he might say, but his namesake's words were often fitting for the situations he found himself in. He had never stopped believing in God, like some of the folks at his old church seemed to believe, and he trusted his heavenly Father the same today as he did all those years ago when his world was shaken. He just lost sight of the end. He knew in his heart and soul that there was a plan for everything, but he couldn't reconcile the loss of his sister with that knowledge. She had been his best friend and cheerleader since the day they were born, and when she died, something in him went with her, including his ability to talk to his Holy Father.

He had left the church at the same time, no longer able to praise God in the comfort and warmth of the sanctuary. Now he was more comfortable fulfilling his purpose and praising his father while walking through crumbling and broken cities, talking with the downtrodden, and, in rare occasions, sitting in a cheap motel room after detoxing.

Sitting in the bed, his head leaned up against the wall. David thought about the first time he had ever desired to take someone's pain. He was fifteen and had the gift of empathy. The gift was so strong when he was connected with Christ that he could literally feel the pain of those around him, physical and emotional. It was hard at that age, feeling things he had no experience with. Depression in a friend that nearly destroyed David, despair from a classmate that later admitted to physical abuse from her father, and a constant pain in his lower back whenever he was with his grandmother, who died of bone cancer in her lower spine some years later.

All of these things he felt vividly, while living a comfortable if not charmed, young life. His parents never quite understood what drove his often erratic mood swings and took drastic measures to relieve him of the "unbalance" they suspected as the cause. Their final attempt to fix him lead to a youth pastor who took the time to understand. That same youth pastor, Caleb, taught him to use discernment to understand the root of his unfamiliar emotions. They spent the next three years praying together and building an unshakable faith, probably the reason David didn't walk away from God when he walked away from the church.

When Caleb was thirty-one, he lost his firstborn son in a freak accident, and for the first time, David prayed to take the turmoil that shook his friend. By the power of the Holy Spirit, he was able to do so. In this case, the pain wasn't fully removed, but the load was lightened, allowing the pastor to mourn with his family, without falling into a relationship ruining despair. Caleb was the only person from the old church to stay in contact. Not anybody's fault, they just didn't understand the way it felt to feel their pity for his loss.

Of all the feelings he had felt in this lifetime, pity was the one he could stand the least. Even now, all these years later, if he ran into someone from the church, they immediately did the cocked head, furrowed eyebrow, pity look, followed always by, "Oh, how are you, what's it been [XX] years?" He despised it. He was pretty sure they all thought he had gone off the deep end, like camel hair robe, locust eating, John the Baptist, type crazy. In reality, he had focused completely on God's plan and purpose, diving head first into the waves to help save the drowning from themselves. So maybe he had gone off the deep end. If so, Caleb was his reminder to breath.

As if on cue, his phone began to vibrate. "Caleb" flashed on the screen.

"If I believed in telepathy, I'd swear you have it," David answered.

"They call that brotherly love, a spiritual connection," Caleb responded, laughing.

"Oh, is that what that is? I was just thinking about you. It's about 3:00 a.m. here, so what's that, five there?"

"Yeah, too early to be up normally, but if you start thinking about me and I feel it, that means you need me to come get you and bring you back to reality. What's it been, three months? And where are you? Your mom won't stop talking about Thanksgiving plans, and she is not happy you haven't RSVP'd."

"She does realize it's over two months away, right?"

"Like that matters, she started asking about you like a month ago. Seriously, where are you?"

"Spokane," David answered, taking a long drink of water.

"As in Washington?"

"Yeah."

"How'd you get to Washington?"

"Who knows how this happens. A little bit of walking, some climbing. Sometimes, the bus, you know. Met a guy at the zoo in Nebraska, then an old man in Billings, and then April a few nights ago. This was a new one, brother."

"What do you mean?" Caleb sounded intrigued. "And since when do you share names?"

"I can't explain it. First, it's my first heroin addiction, not fun, but more than that, this girl's special. Like I said, I can't explain it."

"Oh, a special girl, eh? You know I have some contacts in Coeur d' Alene, right? Do you need me to get you a place to stay and a ticket home? Having a lady in your life doesn't seem like a smart move right now."

"No, not yet. There's something that feels unfinished, and it's not like that with April. Who knows if I'll ever even see her again."

"You sure?"

"Yeah. Besides, this little hotel is starting to feel like home."

"You know, you're crazy right?"

"Brother, that's what they tell me. I'll call you when it's finished. Love you."

He broke the connection.

She awoke with a start. Frantic to find herself tangled in the bedsheets in the darkness. It took her a minute to realize she was in her room, safe from the nightmare that woke her. It was him again, but this time, it was different. Every night this week, she had dreamt of him. Before, the dreams were pleasant memories of meeting him. The way his size had scared her at first. Alone on the deserted street, he had seemed formidable, threatening, but she was comforted almost immediately by his voice. Both in the moment, she had actually met him and in the dreams that followed.

Years of experience taught her to be weary and untrusting of strangers, especially men, yet somehow, even in her dreams, he was able to shake those feelings from her with his calm demeanor. Most of her dreams reenacted the meeting, over and over again. Visions of herself desperately trying to look more presentable, her reflection in the bathroom mirror at Phil's appearing more as a stranger than how she saw herself. She dreamt of the moment he had kissed her forehead and taken her addiction. Each night, with repetition of the dream, she felt more comfortable with him. Felt herself wanting to know more about him.

This time, she woke from the dream afraid and worried. Not for herself, but for him, David. She had dreamt that he was trapped in a box, covered by a large chain, and somehow, she knew she had to get him out of it, or his fate might change forever. Lost and trapped in the box.

She looked at the clock on her end table, 3:16 a.m. Too early to do anything now, but she knew she would have to find him. She laid in bed annoyed by her inability to sleep. His face kept flashing in her mind, tense and riddled with anxiety. The longer she lay awake, the more difficult she found it to reconcile the emotions he displayed in the dream with the man she had met just days before.

Sighing, she rolled over, wishing there was a TV in her room. She would take the endless stream of infomercials common to this time of morning, over the endless flashes of dream that raced through her mind. Then she remembered, there was a Bible app she could download. She had never read the Bible, but she had heard verses that she liked. Maybe something in there would ease her mind.

Once downloaded, only minutes later, she opened the app, pausing; where would she even begin? "God," she whispered, "if you're really there, can you just tell me where to go, what to read?" She opened the app, closed her eyes, and scrolled through the different books. When she opened her eyes, her finger sat on Ecclesiastes. She clicked. Numbers appeared, the chapters she assumed, randomly selecting three. More numbers. *Who would have thought there's so much to this?* she thought, clicking 1. Words displayed on the bright screen. "There is a time for everything, and a season for every activity under the heavens: A time to be born and a time to die, a time to plant and a time to uproot, a time to kill and a time to heal…"

He stood in the shower, steam so thick it was like a sauna. At least, there was one good thing about this place, hot water and plenty of it pouring over him. He let the water run over his aching muscles. He had climbed mountains without this level of muscle ache afterwards.

He was thinking about Hope again. Missing her, the ache in his heart almost blocking out the pain that flooded his body. It was coming up on seven years since she had died. Seven years from the day he wasn't able to save her. He felt anger begin to rise up in his spirit. A storm threatening to drag him under and toss him into a sea of despair. He pulled himself back quoting another of his favorite verses; this one from Exodus. "The Lord will fight for you, you must only be still." He spoke the verse over and over, until his heart began to relent. As the heat softened the knots in his muscle, the word softened the knots in his heart.

He dried off quickly and dressed out of the backpack, the only belongings he carried on his travels. He wasn't expecting to stay this long, and his wardrobe was in dire need of a cleaning. After stuffing his clothes back in the backpack, he googled the nearest laundromat. The compass has limited use. There were a few within ten miles, but only one caught his attention. It was a little over five miles from his hotel and only half a mile from Phil's. He felt a strange yearning in his heart to see April again. Maybe, although he hoped not, he could find somebody who knew her.

He glanced down at his watch. It was shortly after nine thirty, assuming the walk took about two hours and leaving half an hour to get his laundry started and walk to Phil's. It should be about noon by the time he arrived. He hadn't thought to check the business hours, since he never actually considered returning, but noon felt like a safe bet. He put in his earbuds and left the room.

When her eyes fluttered open several hours later, she was filled with an unusual sense of calm, accompanied by a feeling of expectancy. She couldn't pinpoint exactly when she had decided, but at some point, during her Bible reading, she just knew that she had to find him.

After showering, she sat on her bed with her makeup bag beside her. Tempted at first to apply it as she normally would, the heavy dark eyeliner and lipstick were the style with her normal crowd, instead she settled on earthier tones, mascara, and a clear gloss, rather than her normal dark red lipstick.

She thought about the comment David had made about her name, April, like spring and new life. Maybe this was her chance at something new; she didn't know what that meant or how to get it, not to mention the mysterious God he spoke of, the one she had prayed to for the first time ever only hours earlier. Was it really possible that some divine man in the sky—creator of the universe—would use someone? David not only thought so but was apparently a living proof of it. She hadn't had a fix since that day. Not a drug, drink, or even a cigarette. Even more shockingly, she hadn't even been tempted. She had gone a few days without in the past, but either hung out with friends partying and gave into their offers or succumbed to the pains of withdrawal.

Her first few days away from the group had been surprisingly peaceful, despite the constant nagging of her phone. Calls, texts, social media comments all asking where she was. Eventually, they had all stopped. All except for Kyle D., her longtime dealer and borderline stalker. April was pretty sure Kyle was harmless but kept a safe distance between the two of them at parties. He had texted and called at least once every day this week, leaving voicemails she didn't care to listen to and generic texts about "something new." He wasn't the type to leave a comment online, too paranoid for that.

The rest of her "friends" had stopped after three days. They all probably assumed she was dead or behind bars. She wasn't the first to disappear from the group, who were quick to forget old friendships, and she certainly wouldn't be the last.

Her mother had even taken a few days off work to reconnect, which, aside from the mall tension, had gone well so far. Maye was never easy to get along with. She had always been quick to anger and unable to see past her own nose. That's probably what caused April's father to leave. Well, that or the constant stream of pills and booze, Maye's self-prescribed remedy for her self-diagnosed crippling anxiety.

When Maye was able to stay clean, she had actually been a halfway decent mom. Even making school lunches and filling the fridge with the latest health food craze. Unfortunately, more often than not, she was hungover and unable to put on her own clothes, leaving April to fend for herself.

Even before her father left, April's parents had slept in different beds most nights. Not that she blamed her dad. Outside of short bursts of sobriety, Maye's room always smelled like a sock left in a car in the heat over summer. Dad worked nights anyways, so the off schedule allowed him to sleep, while leaving Maye free to party and April taking care of herself. She pulled herself out of her childhood memories as she pulled the towel off her wet hair, cold drops dripping on her shoulders and back. *What to do with this?* she thought.

Her hair was dark with a hint of auburn in the right light and straighter than plywood. Usually, she used excessive amounts of gel, back combing, and temporary color to spice it up, but today, she decided to add some Moroccan oil and let it dry. She had been up for too long anyways and could feel her stomach growling. She decided to make breakfast for the two of them.

Downstairs, she started bacon in the oven, prepped the coffee pot, scrambled eggs, and peeled some oranges, humming (surprising even to her) "Amazing Grace," a song she'd heard only a handful of times in her life, mostly at funerals. She poured herself a cup of coffee, set the oven to warm, and put the meal on the racks to stay warm until her mother woke. She sat at the table, enjoying the warm glow of the sun on her face through the windows.

Waiting, she glanced at the clock every few minutes. She had been sitting at the table for nearly thirty minutes, and it was now past nine thirty. "Oh god, not again," she muttered, leaving the sun's soft touch to wake Maye from what she assumed was a pill/wine stupor.

Back up the stairs, she knocked lightly while pushing the door inward. "Mom," she whispered, "Mom, are you up?" A deep "huh" stopped April in her tracks. *Oh great, she's got company*, she thought. All patience lost, she strolled to the window, tripping over who knows what, and jerked back the curtains. A stream of light poured into the room over a naked man and her (thankfully) covered mother.

"Okay, Maye, time to clean up and oh my gosh, what died in here? You smell like farts and moldy cheese. Ugh, get up." A small part of her felt guilty. She had been on the other side of rude awakenings. Unfortunately for Maye and the naked man, her empathy for the situation and soon-to-come hangover pains were overridden by her knowledge that if they didn't get up now, they wouldn't get up today. Her stomach growled, reminding her of the breakfast still waiting in the oven, their muffled groans not enough to convince her they were getting up.

She walked stiffly to the bathroom and filled a large plastic tub found under the sink with the coldest water the faucet was willing to produce. She thought about running downstairs to get ice but realized that was just spiteful. Marching back down the hall, she sang loudly the few words she could remember. "Amazing Grace, how sweet the sound, that saved a wretch like meeeeeeeeee. I once was lost but now am found was blind but now I seeeeeee." She dumped the bucket on the sleeping grinch and her gentlemen caller, giggling hysterically.

"What the hell?" Maye yelled, shooting up from the covers.

"Sorry, Mom, you missed your friendly wakeup call and breakfast is ready. Please ask your, um, friend…to leave, put on your robe and join me for breakfast."

"April, get out. Marv, get up, and out."

"Okay, Mom, but I'll be back in twenty minutes with ice if you're not down, do you want sugar and creamer—"

"April out!" her mother roared.

Nineteen minutes later, Marv was out the door and Maye stood over the table fuming with bloodshot eyes.

"What on earth is wrong with you?" she demanded.

"Good morning to you too, Mom. Would you like some eggs and bacon? It's been sitting in the oven for about an hour now, so hopefully it's edible. I'd be happy to make you a plate and get you coffee."

Maye sat in the chair with an audible *hmph*. "What was that about, April?"

"I thought you were clean, Mom," April replied, slamming the half-filled plate against the counter."

"I am clean, Marv and I were just up late."

"Don't even try it! You do realize I'm not the fifteen-year-old kid anymore, right? Like, I won't fall for the lies. I've used them, Mom. I've *lived* them." She prepared herself for the oncoming fight. Maye would yell about how April abandoned her, just like April's father had. Then she would go on about her anxiety and how she didn't trust doctors, and how as a child her parents had been terrible to her. How April couldn't understand, maybe Maye hadn't been the best mother, but she was a better parent than she ever had. The lines repeated over and over in April's head. Memories of the arguments that sent her out the doors all those years ago. She prepared herself for the battle.

"You're right."

"No, Mom." She started, before realizing what Maye said. She was too shocked to continue. Not once in her life had she heard her mother say those words. Picking up the plates, she asked, "Are you okay?"

"Yeah."

Walking to the table, April set the plate and cup down in front of her mother. "Do you want to talk about it?"

"I guess."

He thought about April as he walked. This was new territory. He had never gone looking for them before, always trusting the compass, fulfilling his role, and moving on. He never wanted them to consider him a hero or a healer. He had seen and knew all too well the hysteria that came with that sort of name. He let God pick them, took what he was meant to take, and never looked back. But not now. The pull in his heart to find her was almost as strong as the compass had been the night he had. This was one of the rare times he wished that he had some level of control over the thing, but he knew it was best to let God guide him.

He felt the fingers of doubt crawling along his mind. Maybe Caleb was right. Was this even allowed? It's not like he'd ever sat down and wrote out a job aid for this, he just trusted God. The fingers became claws as he wrestled to find truth in his thoughts.

"And the peace of God, which transcends all understanding, will guard your hearts and our minds, in Jesus Christ." He repeated another of his go-to verses, this one from Philippians, out loud for several blocks. Until the unease began to fade. Once at the laundromat, he determined that going to Phil's was acceptable. If God intended for him to interact with April again, maybe she would be there. If not, he would move along. "Don't overthink it." He told himself, starting the washer in the empty room; the only other person an employee too engrossed in his cell phone to take notice of him.

After the machine was running, he quickly walked the ten blocks to Phil's, noting how run down the area was in the light of day. Entering the bar, he paused to assess the lunch patrons. Although slightly more occupied than his last visit, it was clear that neither noon nor midnight were popular times for the dive, at least not on Monday night or early Tuesday morning. Part of him hoped there was an afternoon crowd, for Phil's sake.

He picked the same stool as before and watched as the bartender, an older lady with "Bee" displayed on her name badge, handed drinks to a couple a few seats away. Walking toward him, she asked, "What can I get you, hon?" The pungent smell of cigarette smoke hitting him before she stood across from him.

"Coffee please," David said, shaking away his second odd desire to smoke.

"I'll have to brew a fresh pot, might take a minute, that okay?"

"Absolutely, thank you."

"Do you want a menu?"

His look of surprise must have been one familiar to her, as she chuckled and said, "Yeah, yeah. I know, not the most obvious choice for food, but it ain't that bad, just stay away from the beef."

His stomach growled at the thought of a full meal. He had been living off prepackage protein packs and Gatorade for the past several days. "All right, Miss Bee, you've convinced me. What's your favorite thing on the menu?"

"I'm partial to the club sandwich. It comes with a side of your choice."

"Sold. I'll take the club, with fries and ranch if you've got it."

"Coming right up."

Bee was right. The food arrived just a few minutes later, along with the fresh brewed coffee. He assumed the quick service was due to the lack of customers.

"Here you go, hon," she said, placing the plate and coffee in front of him. "Holler if you need anything else."

He pulled his phone from this pocket, opened the Bible app, and selected a random book and verse to read from. His usual action if he was sure there was something he needed to know but wasn't sure what it was. While it wasn't foolproof, he had often heard the Lord's voice and will in this way. Landing in Ecclesiastes 3, he began to read:

> There is a time for everything, and a season for every activity under the heavens: A time to be born and a time to die, a time to plant and a time to uproot, a time to kill and a time to heal, a time to tear down and a time to build, a time to weep and a time to laugh, a time to mourn and a time to dance, a time to scatter stones and a time to gather them, a time to embrace and a time to refrain from embracing, a time to search and a time to give up, a time to keep and a time to throw away, a time to tear and a time to mend, a time to be silent and a time to speak, a time to love and a time to hate, a time for war and a time for peace. What do the workers gain from their toil? I have seen the burden God has laid on the human race. He has made everything beautiful in its time. He has also set eternity in the human heart; yet no one can fathom what God has done from beginning to end. I know that there is noth-

ing better for people than to be happy and to do good while they live. That each of them may eat and drink, and find satisfaction in their toil—this is the gift of God. I know that everything God does will endure forever; nothing can be added to it and nothing taken from it. God does it so that people will fear him.

Whatever is has already been, and what will be has been before; and God will call the past to account. And I saw something else under the sun: In the place of judgement—wickedness was there, in the place of justice—wickedness was there. I said to myself, "God will bring into judgement both the righteous and the wicked, for there will be a time for every activity, a time to judge every deed." I also said to myself, "As for humans, God tests them so that they may see they are like the animals. Surely the fate of human beings is like that of the animals; the same fate awaits them both: As one dies, so dies the other. All have the same breath, humans have no advantage over animals. Everything is meaningless. All go to the same place; all come from dust, and to dust all return. Who knows if the human spirit rises upward and if the spirit of the animal goes down into the earth? So, I saw there

> is nothing better for a person to enjoy their work, because that is their lot. For who can bring them to see what will happen after them.

He read over the chapter several times, pondering what it meant for him, here, now. He didn't believe in coincidence in his work, especially when it came to listening to God, and although he'd never been one to ask for signs, it was not new to him to receive them, and he was certain he was brought to this chapter for a reason. A change was about to come. He thought he would be heading home, but it looked like he might have another job to do first.

The bell on the door chimed, drawing his head up. He was hoping to see April and felt a ping of disappointment when a young blonde entered instead.

Bee took the woman's order and walked toward the kitchen, asking if he needed anything as she passed. David considered asking about April, remembering that Phil was supposedly her uncle, but quickly let the idea slide, instead responding, "Just the check please, ma'am."

"You got it, kid. Now forgive me for overstepping, but I've been doing this job a long while, and I noticed your face changed just a minute ago. You look tense. Everything all right?"

He laughed heartily at her question. "Yes, Miss Bee, I'm fine. Just work I suppose."

She shrugged and waved her arm around the room, as if inviting him to take in the sight. "Trust me, kid, I know how disappointing work can be. Take it from this old gal, you'll be okay. Things always work out in the end, even if you can't see it past the linoleum and florescent lights."

"My dear Miss Bee, you just might be an angel." He laughed again, pulling cash from his wallet to cover the bill and a generous tip. "God bless you, ma'am."

With that, he walked toward the door.

"So, what happened?" she asked after several minutes of awkward silence.

"I just don't know who to be now," Maye answered through a mouth full of eggs.

"What do you mean?"

"I mean, I was never great. Never a good mom, not a good wife, but after you left, people stopped looking at me like I had a problem. They started to pity you once the rumors got around. I wasn't happy, and I've spent the past six plus years terrified for the life you were living, never knowing if I would see you again, but I was also relieved. Like I wasn't responsible for you anymore." Maye pushed her empty plate away.

"Oh," was the only response April could muster.

"So, who are you now? When you came back, I was happy. So happy that you were alive, and then, when you said that you weren't addicted anymore, that this random man David had taken it, I thought, 'What the hell, let her have it.' But I didn't believe it, April. Come on, it's insane. I waited and waited for you to go through withdrawal. I thought if you did that, maybe you'd need me, and I was ready to be there, to be your mom, and to help guide you through it, but these past few days, it's like you aren't even you. Who are you now?"

April sat, stunned. She didn't know how to answer. At first, it was weird. For so long, it was just the norm for her to party. Feeling lonely? There's a drug for that. Feeling down in the dumps, maybe a little depressed? Here, have this. Didn't sleep well last night, snort this; you'll wake right up. She hadn't had to live with herself for so long, it was an awkward and somewhat uncomfortable transition.

Those first few days, she hadn't known what to do. What do normal people do when they aren't working and are just around? (Bored, I got something for that). She'd googled more about the Bible, sitting at the table while Maye worked on crossword puzzles and had learned some about the man Jesus, using the Bible app she had finally downloaded last night. They had even watched some movies and TV shows. But through all of it, she still felt like there was something missing. Like when David had taken her addiction, it had left a big empty space in her life. He was right when he told her it might hurt. It just wasn't the way she had expected it to.

It was almost like she was expecting some physical pain disconnecting her from it. Instead, she felt an odd sadness to see it go. Not exactly to see the addiction go, but it did leave her feeling a little unsure of exactly who she was supposed to be now. Nearly seven years of her life, all of her adult years, had been spent looking for the next high. She always had a purpose, even if it wasn't the best of purposes. Now, well at least until last night, she wasn't sure what was supposed to come next.

Despite all of it, it hadn't crossed her mind that she was different, or might seem like a different person to someone on the outside looking in. She felt like herself, same old April, just without the need to hide or seek refuge for whatever emotion she was unwilling to deal with.

"April?" her mother asked in anticipation.

Realizing she'd been silent for several minutes, she answered, "I don't know, Mom, but I think I'm free."

"April, that doesn't even make sense. Free from what?" her mother said, exasperated.

"That night with David, he said, 'In the name of Jesus, your chains are broken.'"

"What chains, April, you don't have any chains. Even if you did, how did they break, and who is this random man that thinks he can break them?"

"I don't know, Mom, but I think I have to find out. I think he can tell me, but there's more," she hesitated, "I think he might be in trouble."

"Again, what do you mean? From the way you described him, it seems like he can take care of himself."

"It's not like that. Not like somebody is going to kidnap him, it's more like there's something coming that might destroy him."

"That's a little dramatic, don't you think?"

April thought about telling more about her dream but decided against it. "Maybe it is, Mom, but can I really risk it? Like you said, who am I now? If he can just go around taking people's 'stuff,' why can't he tell me what comes next?"

"So, you want to what? Chase him down, ask him what? When we talked about this yesterday, you called me crazy. Besides, what does he even know about you, April? I thought you said he was just gone. How will you even find him."

"I don't know, Mom, but don't you think I have to try?"

"Why can't you just be content with where you are now? You're free, right? Can't you just start living like a normal person?"

"What does normal look like, Mom? And no, how could I? You think this is the type of thing that happens every day? Maybe that's part of what I need to know. Why me?"

"It just doesn't seem smart to go chasing down a man like that."

"A man that tries to help people?"

"A man that finds random females on the streets and talks them into letting him take something from them."

"You could try to be a little more positive about this, you know? This could be something, Mom."

Maye shoveled the last scoop of scrambled eggs into her mouth, "Okay, you're right. Just promise me you'll be careful. I just got you back, and I'm not ready to lose you again."

"Oh, hi," David said, pulling the door back to leave Phil's. "I wasn't expecting you there." He stepped politely to the side to let the short elderly woman enter Phil's. *Not even a thank you*, he thought. *Kids these days.*

Part of him was almost happy he didn't find April, what would he even say? "Hey, remember me? The weird guy that chased you down via brain arrow?" This wasn't the type of thing that could easily be discussed. After he met them and let the Lord do the work, that was it. Caleb was the only person he had ever taken from and continued to interact with, the only one who knew. And even though he didn't fully understand it, Caleb had always trusted that David had a handle on it, admitting more than once though that David might be in over his head.

As for good old mom and pop, they'd basically assumed he had lost it after Hope's death. Assuming he was on some Batman-esque mission to save the broken in a way, he wasn't able to save his sister. To be fair, there was probably some truth to that. He realized suddenly that he had walked several blocks past the laundromat. He turned on his heels and backtracked to the small worn-down building, thinking to himself how odd it was that he was thinking of Hope so much, especially after pushing down memories of her for so many years.

Once in the still empty building, he nodded to the employee, who was still too engrossed by his cell phone to notice or respond and walked to the machine that held all the clothes he brought with him, minus, of course, the ones he was wearing. He moved the dripping clothes from the washer to the dryer. After starting the dry cycle, he settled into the uncomfortable plastic chair and opened his Bible app. He stared at the screen, unsure of where to begin. He thought about what he had read in Ecclesiastics earlier and felt again the weight of disappointment settle on his heart. He had been positive that April would be at Phil's. It just felt so right that he would see her again. He needed to know more about her. Maybe this was some sort of test. He wasn't sure what it was, but either way, he felt certain he had failed it. In any case, his mind was too unfocused to try and read, so instead he put in his earbuds and selected a playlist of old hymns. He leaned back in the chair and closed his eyes as "The Old Rugged Cross" played. When his mind was too preoccupied to read, hymns always settled his spirit. *Peace be still*, he thought.

The songs continued to do work in his spirit. He felt the calmest he had been in days but couldn't loosen the feeling of anticipation. It wasn't new to him. There were a few years where he kept minimal interaction with anybody, including Caleb, and during those years, he had often felt a yearning or anticipation that didn't make sense to him. Generally, he would chalk it up to loneliness and call Caleb, who was quick to invite him home and remind him of all the loved ones waiting for him. It just didn't feel like home anymore.

A few years after her death, he had finally gone back, ready to face them and whatever backlash might come from his sudden exit from the O'Luain household. To his surprise, there was none. His mother welcomed him with open arms, thrilled and emotional (as much as she was able to show) to have her only living child returned to her. The whole deal felt like a Hallmark channel Christmas special. He didn't doubt his parent's love for him but always felt like there was a dark cloud of "unspokenness" hovering over the household.

He stayed for as long as he could, but eventually, the constant smiles and family dinners were overwhelming. It was as if they were trying to recreate what had been when Hope's joy had filled the house; he couldn't handle it. After about two weeks, he left again. This time purchasing a prepaid cellphone to keep with him and giving his mother the number. His father shook his hand when he left, disappointment clinging to his voice like cobwebs to the corner. At first, he had tried to explain why he had to leave, but they would never understand and he could never stay as long as they tried to maintain a façade. He was unwilling then and still unwilling now to live in a place where the past was scrubbed of its reality, and time was frozen to avoid the sadness that came in the dark.

He felt for his mother, truly he did, but no part of him could stand to face her when she was unable to face the truth. They put on the right face, the right mask. They smiled and laughed heartily while keeping pleasant company with the pastor and his family, but they never, not even once, allowed themselves to grieve for her death. That unspoken grief weighed heavily in his heart and in his mind, making their smiles seem like plastic.

An unsatisfied air of unfinished settled again on his heart. He tried to push it away, as he had so many times before, but that feeling took the place of anticipation and left him between an emotional rock and hard place. He turned the music up on his phone and tried again to listen to the words of the hymns that played.

As the song came to its end, he felt cool air coming from the front door.

After another half hour of calming Maye down, ensuring that she would be careful and promising to check in periodically, April tucked her mother in for a nap, cleaned the dishes, and paced the living room arguing with herself.

"I must be crazy. Where would I even start? It's not like I can just walk around town hoping to bump into him. One of us doesn't have a nice little people tracker brain arrow. Besides, I sat with him in a dark bar for like an hour. I might not even recognize him." As she said it, she knew it was a lie. She would no sooner forget David's face than she would forget the look on her father's when said he was leaving. No, those were two moments in her life that had changed it forever and two faces she would never forget.

She paused, stuck between the decision to stay at the house and cater to her mother's hangover and the decision to take a chance and go on an adventure in the city. The adventure won. If nothing else, she could stop by Phil's and get a Rueben. "Oh my god, Phil's!" she said out loud, followed by, "Oops, I mean oh my *gosh*, I think that's better." She knew it was a long shot, but if there was even a chance he might be there, she had to try. She grabbed the keys from the peg by the door and began her trip.

The drive to Phil's was a quick one. Thanks to the 2008 economic decline, the streets were practically empty. A few businesses had somehow managed to stay afloat in the area, a record store, at least two mechanics, a laundromat, thrift store, and of course, Phil's, but most of the buildings were boarded up and empty.

She parked in the front and walked slowly toward the door. This was the first time she had visited a bar since that night, and she anticipated the familiar longing and need that might take hold when she entered, so she stood outside, staring at the door like it was a gateway standing between her and a monster ready to snatch up her soul. Who knows, maybe it was. She stood until she was startled from her thoughts by a little old lady leaving with a to-go bag.

"Oh, excuse me," she said, stepping aside. No response from granny. Even though it had only been a few short hours since breakfast, the strong scent of french fries lured her into the building.

She walked pensively to the bar and sat in the same stool as that night. Bee, her favorite bartender, smiled as she sat.

"Well, hey there, sugar," Bee said, placing the little white napkin in front of her. "The usual?"

"No, not today, Bee. I'm thinking maybe soda and a plate of fries with ranch."

"Sure. You kids these days are something else, eating that ranch sauce like it was sent from the very gates of heaven. Some other young guy, sitting right in that stool next to you, practically bathed in the stuff." Laughing, Bee took the order to the kitchen and returned only moments later with the soda. "So, what brings you down today? We don't usually see you this early."

"Actually, I was hoping to see someone here. I met him the other night, but I have a feeling this isn't his usual crowd," April answered, taking a sip of the soda, which tasted surprisingly different without the somewhat bitter taste of whiskey.

"Well, what's he like?" Bee asked, wiping the bar with a dingy cloth.

"Um, he's a big guy, like football player type big. When I met him, he was dressed well. Not like all fancy, but you know clean."

"Actually"—Bee stopped wiping—"the ranch fellow who came in earlier was like that. Real handsome guy, nice sweater, not the type we usually see. I'll be honest, I was a bit smitten myself."

"What?" April nearly jumped off the stool. "Bee, it might be him. What did he say?"

"Not much really. He was polite though, said something about work. He was reading something on his phone, then got this real disappointed look on his face when a little blonde came through the door. You know me, can't keep to my own thoughts, so I asked him what was botherin' him, and he said his job. Didn't say what it was, just that it was getting him down. He did say I was an angel though, and then, get this, 'God bless you.' Can you believe it? That's not something you hear in a place like this."

"Bee, that's definitely him," April exclaimed. "Did he say where he was going? I have to go." The stool toppled, threatening to fall as she leapt hurriedly off it.

"No, but you just missed him. He hasn't been gone more than twenty minutes. That stool's probably still warm. Don't run off just yet, let me put your fries in a bag and get you a to-go cup for your soda."

"Thank you, Bee. How much do I owe you?"

"This one's on me, hon, just be sure to come back and tell me if you found him."

Moments later, she was heading for the door when she paused, looked back, and said, "Hey, Bee, God bless you, truly."

Once outside, she stopped again, not sure which way to go. "Okay, God," she said, "I'm not entirely sure how praying is supposed to go, but I'm going to try. Can you help me find him? Show me the way?" She stood waiting, before turning left and walking down the street. After several minutes passing by empty store fronts, the clutch of disappointment began to cling to her heart. This was madness. Spokane was a big city, and at this time of day, one could get far in twenty minutes. She felt like an idiot. He had probably taken a cab back to wherever it was he was staying. She was about to turn back but paused as her eyes caught a neon Open sign flashing across the street, in the window of the laundromat. *Worth a try*, she thought, crossing the empty road.

Opening the door, she was hit with the scent of bleach. It was so strong her eyes began to water. She blinked hard to clear them. When they were finally free of tears, she saw him in the corner.

"It's you," he said.

He almost didn't believe it, thought maybe he had dozed off in his chair, but there she was. She looked different, fresh, almost softened. Her eye makeup was toned down, which to his surprise didn't in any way take away from the brilliant green irises or negate the catlike quality he had noticed those nights ago.

"It's you," was all he could think to say. He wanted to stand up and hug her tightly but worried he might scare her away, so he sat still in the seat and mumbled an awkward, "How?"

"I don't know," April replied, tentatively moving closer, yet remaining out of arm's reach. His desire to embrace her had not yet subsided, so he pushed his hands into his pockets in an attempt to control them.

"I, um, had to find you. I needed to know more about you and your God and how the two of you do what you do." She stood.

"Come, sit." David nodded to the empty seat beside him. "Sorry, they aren't the most comfortable."

She moved into the chair, clutching her bag on her lap. "I don't know where to start."

"We can start wherever you'd like. This is new territory for me."

"What do you mean?"

"I don't usually see the person after it happens."

"Once you take it, or whatever, from someone, you're just gone?"

"That's how it's always been."

"How do you know it works?"

"Didn't it?" He gestured at her.

"Well, yeah, but you see me. If you didn't, how would you know?"

"Faith is the confidence that what we hope for will actually happen. It gives us assurance about the things we cannot see."

"I think I've heard that before," she said, cocking her head in thought. "But what does it mean?"

"It's in Hebrews in the Bible. Basically, it means that I have confidence enough in God to believe that what is meant to happen happens."

"You don't control it?"

"No, but technically it's not me taking it."

"Who then?"

"The Holy Spirit."

"And then what, it's just gone?"

"Well, kind of."

She stood up frustrated and began pacing. "I don't understand, and it seems like you're being intentionally vague."

"Truthfully"—he fought the urge to stand with her—"I don't always understand either, and I *am* being vague. Not many people care to know or are even capable of having any sort of understanding."

The now familiar fire returned to her eyes, as she stopped mid stride, turning on her heels to face him again. "Are you saying I'm dumb?"

He sighed, leaned back in the chair, and threw his arms up in defeat. "No, April, I'm not saying you're dumb. It has nothing to do with you or your intellect. Just the reality of it versus the perception people tend to have for these things. People tend to get the whole 'faith healer' mentality. You see it all the time. Some guy shows up out of the blue, says he can heal people, starts charging people twenty bucks at the door, speaks some mumbo jumbo and disappears. This isn't like that. I'm not saying healers don't exist, they do, but I'm not gifted with that."

"What are you gifted with?"

"I told you, taking."

She continued pacing in front of him. "You're doing it again, the vague thing."

Resting his elbows on his knees, he looked up at her. "Fine. I'll tell you whatever you want to know."

She sat beside him, looking intently into his eyes, almost causing him to break his gaze. "How does it work?"

"Which part?"

"When you actually take it."

Sighing again, he decided it was all or nothing. This is what she wanted, right? "Well, first, let's be clear, I don't take it. I don't have that type of authority. The Holy Spirit moves it to me."

Her eyebrows furrowed as she struggled to understand. "Moves it to you?"

"Yes. It's not technically gone when I take it. Whatever it is has to be resolved."

Her eyes widened. "So, then you?"

"Yes. Everything taken becomes my burden."

"Like all of it?" Catlike, she was back to pacing.

"Yes, but generally to a lesser extent."

"Not as bad?"

"Sometimes. I don't have a point of reference. I think it just subsides faster. It's easier for me to break the chains, since I don't have the historical knowledge that led to them in the first place."

"Is that what you meant that night?"

"Yes, your addiction and the chains binding it to you physically became mine."

She stopped again, a look of panic spreading across her face. "You mean, you went through withdrawal?"

"Yes."

She sat suddenly, this time on the floor at his feet. Staring up at him, unable to form a thought, she muttered, "But how?"

"I guess just like you would have, only without the habit of using to bait and trap me again."

Her head was dropped as she pondered. Several minutes passing before she looked up again, tear stains on her cheeks. "Was it awful?"

David chuckled despite himself, attempting to suppress the noise in this throat, fearing it may cause her to flee. "Well, it wasn't fun."

A thin smile formed on her mouth as she responded, "No, it never is. How many?"

"How many what?"

"How many people have you taken from."

"Dozens."

"And they always let you?"

"No, not always. I guess that's the only time it doesn't really work. Some people are too stuck to their pain to let me take it. I can't just force them to give it up. They have to be willing to. For some, that piece of them has become part of who they are, the thought of losing that identity is too painful for them to see their true identity in Christ, free from their bondage."

"Then what do you do?"

"Nothing."

"You just leave them?"

"Like I said, I can't force them to let me take it. God opens the door. They have to choose to walk through it."

"That seems awful. Just walking away from them."

"It's never been easy. I always do my best to convince them, and I pray for them and hope that if it's his will, God will lead me back to them. God gave man the freedom to choose. If they choose not to accept what's offered, I have to respect that."

She nodded, although he could tell she was still struggling with the fact that he had to leave some. "When, or um, how did it start?"

The dryer chimed.

"My clothes are done and that's a long story. How about we find coffee, and I'll tell you all about it. Just not at Phil's."

"No, not at Phil's." She agreed.

She watched him as he removed his clothes from the dryer, folded them, and placed them neatly in his backpack. Who was this man? He claimed to be without authority but moved with the strength and confidence of a lion. He was right though, she didn't understand what any of this meant. The basic concept of his gift yes, but the actuality of willingly taking the burdens of someone you didn't even know? She needed to know him more, to understand his gift and the God who gave it to him. David glanced up, caught her staring and smiled. She felt a warm flush on her face and quickly looked away.

"Are you ready?" he asked, slinging the bag over his shoulder.

She nodded, asking, "Where should we go?"

"This is your town, girl. Lead the way." He pushed the door back for her.

Walking through, she asked, "What? No compass to a coffee house?" through giggles.

With a hearty laugh, he answered, "Unfortunately no, it's not a GPS."

"There might be a little mom and pop place a few miles up, if it's still there. I can drive."

"Let's walk. The sun is out. It's a beautiful day, and to be honest, after being cooped up in the hotel and that awful bed for days, it's nice to get some fresh air."

"Why were you stuck in bed? Were you sick?" Then it hit her and she dropped her head.

"Oh yeah. That."

"Cheer up, girl, the past is the past and now it's behind us. To the future, lead the way."

She took the lead, having never felt safer in her life than with the mountain of a man walking beside her. As they walked in comfortable silence, she began to think about what his life must have been like. He seemed so isolated, yet somehow not lonely. So strong but gentle. So confident yet humble. What were his parents like? She imagined they at least shared a bed. His mom probably even made brownies, the type from scratch, not a two-dollar box.

He was probably even a jock in high school, captain of the football team, the type of jerk that picked on girls like her. Made fun of the emo kids and bullied the band geeks. She felt her fists forming into tight balls as anger rose up in her throat. She must be mad to think a guy like this would have anything to do with her. She realized that her heavy breathing and quickened pace had caused him to look down and watch her as they walked, his pace matching her own.

"You good?" he asked, gently grabbing her arm to slow her down. The warmth of his hand bringing her back from the edge of the rabbit hole she was tediously close to falling in.

"Uh, yeah. I think so. Sorry."

"Do you want to tell me?"

She felt embarrassed, like a child who broke Grandma's favorite vase. "No."

He stopped, removing his hand from her arm. "April, I told you I'd be honest and tell you everything you want to know, but I think this needs to go both ways. Something happened back there. Your whole demeanor changed."

She felt herself begin to pace as he watched, a nervous habit she had had since she was a kid. How could she even say it, *Yeah so sorry I was just imagining the perfect life you must have had with sober parents, Mr. Prom king*. Instead, she said, "I'm not good at honesty."

"Now's as good a time as ever to practice. Let's walk while you tell me, since you're pacing anyways."

"Were you a jerk?" she blurted out, feeling herself shrink away from him.

A shadow of confusion crossed his face, "A jerk?"

"Yeah, you know a bully, the popular jock that picked on smaller weaker kids, prom king type guy."

He laughed as if understanding her thoughts. "I know, I know. I'm a big guy now, but I was a stick until almost seventeen, a late bloomer. Hard to believe it now, huh?"

She nodded in agreement. "Were your parents the happy perfect type? Brady Bunch."

He pondered that for a moment, as though carefully considering his answer. "Yes and no," he finally said. "They were, are good people. They've always been devout Christians, and I appreciate how we were raised, but they also tended to be on the legalistic side. Really focused on right and wrong, driven more by logic and the exact meaning of the word, and the law, rather than the teachings of Jesus. I, on the other hand, have always been more of a feeler, focused on emotions and the relationship between Christ, his disciples, and really anyone he ever met. They weren't really able to connect with me or relate to me on the level I would have liked."

"You have siblings?" April asked.

"What?"

"You said you appreciate how 'we' were raised." She saw his face change, quickly, briefly, something like sorrow sparked in his eyes but only for a second. It reminded her of the man she had seen in her dream, trapped in the box, with the same look of sorrow.

"Goodness, girl," he said with a smile back on his face. I think maybe you've got the gift of counseling. I'm not sure if I've ever met somebody who could so easily get others to open up. We were talking about you."

"It's a learned behavior, keeps the wrong people from prying." April couldn't help but think there was something he wasn't saying and now couldn't remember what she was supposed to be talking about.

"That moment you had back there," David pried.

"Oh, yeah. Um, I guess I was imagining you as this perfect life-ed jock who was a jerk and was thinking about how guys like that used to treat me, almost like I was nothing, worthless." Her fingers began to curl into fists once more. "And I thought, why would someone like you care about someone worthless like me?"

He stopped again, this time with a shocked look on his face. Taking both of her hands in his and looking her straight in the eye, he whispered fiercely, "You are not worthless. That is a lie from the pit of hell. You are a child of God. You are loved and you are accepted. There is an enemy that has kept you chained for who knows how long, but now you've escaped and he wants you back. You cannot believe those lies. Through God's goodness, those chains were broken and your burden was lifted, but only you can choose what happens now. If you accept those lies, you might be willing to pick up those chains again, and there is too much potential in you to let that snake pull you back down."

April shook her head, uncertain of how to respond. Fighting back tears, she said only, "Okay."

He pulled her into a tight embrace saying, "He gives power to the weak and strength to the powerless. Even youths will become weak and tired, and young men will fall in exhaustion. But those who trust in the Lord will find new strength. They will soar high on wings like eagles. They will run and not grow weary. They will walk and not faint."

They walked the last several blocks in silence. His heart aching for her. He had experienced rejection in his own life. He was emotional as a kid and was telling her the truth when he told of the disconnect between himself and his parents. He had even felt worthlessness when taking on the burden of another, but he couldn't begin to fathom what it was like to actually believe that you were worthless.

David knew the tricks of the enemy. He had fought his own battles with the king of lies, some that still haunted him in his sleep. He knew what she was going through. The heaviness that could fall so quickly on one's shoulders when they began to believe the little voices in their head. He wanted to hold her in his embrace forever, to keep away all those voices and protect her from whatever battles were still to come.

As they reached the coffee shop, he pulled the door open for her. Before entering, she paused, looking up at him and said, "I'm glad you were a weak kid." He laughed deeply and followed her through the door.

It was a comfortable looking place, with a French farmhouse sort of vibe. Square white tables were grouped in a corner to the right, opposite from the counter, and books were lined neatly on shelves across from where they stood. Light music played softly in the background, something acoustic.

They walked to the smiling barista and ordered drinks, a black coffee for him and caramel latte for her, before settling into a corner table.

"All right," he said. "Fair's fair. Where do you want to start?"

She pulled her legs up in the chair, crisscross-applesauce style and met his gaze. "Where did it start."

"Ah…yes. That. Well, like I told you, I was a very emotional kid. I had the gift of empathy at a pretty young age, and if I was in sync with God, it was intense. To the extent that I could often feel the physical and emotional pains of others. Sometimes, it was someone I was close to and other times, it was just a glimpse into the mind of someone in the vicinity. In either case, it was oftentimes difficult to cope with. I was too young to understand and think through where the feelings were coming from. Instead, I responded erratically and unpredictably. My parents thought I was suffering from depression and sent me to a therapist. Unfortunately, at that age, I didn't have the words or the wisdom to be able to explain the sudden uncontrollable feelings that would appear out of nowhere, so they put me on antidepressants."

"Seriously," April asked, twisting her coffee cup on the table.

"Yeah. I don't blame them though. It's not like they could know. Based on their understanding of the situation, they were doing what they thought was right."

"Did it work?"

"Kind of, but mostly, it felt like it had the opposite effect. The pills were meant to balance out emotions, level the chemicals in my brain, but I didn't have a chemical imbalance, so instead, they numbed me. I went from having an abundance of emotions, both my own as an adolescent and those of people around me, to having none. There was no balance. It was more like a switch being flipped off. I became cold and drew inward. I stopped spending time with friends and got really comfortable being alone. I think I read through the Bible twice that year, not really taking it in and learning, just reading it with a mechanical brain." He paused to sip his coffee as she rested her face on her palm.

"How did you get out of it?" she asked.

"Well, they started to get really worried," he continued, "like any parent might in that situation and decided to send me to summer camp with the youth group of another church in the area. That's where I met Caleb, the church's youth pastor. I don't know how he did it. The man is a saint and has patience beyond his years. He was young and inexperienced back then but filled with faith like I haven't encountered since. He's like you, with the amazing gift of getting people to talk." He couldn't help but smile as she nodded, listening intently. "Somehow, in that week, he got me to open up. I told him about the things I'd felt—despair, loneliness, physical pains that came out of nowhere. That's when he explained empathy to me. Not in the general sense we hear about, but the truth about the gift of empathy. I'll be honest, there's power in a name, and by giving my 'affliction' a name, I felt empowered to understand the full capacity of it and learn to control it, so to speak."

"So, is that what you do now? Like have supercharged empathy on steroids?"

"Not quite. Empathy was the gift I was given, having the ability to take those pains upon myself was a gift I asked for."

"You asked for this?" she questioned with disbelief written on her face. "Why would you do that?"

"That's the question, isn't it? About three years later, Caleb and I had become extremely close, like brothers. He'd taught me the power of prayer and discernment, having the knowledge to separate my own feelings from those of people around me. I truly owed him everything and still do. So, when his first son was killed in an accident, I couldn't handle seeing him in so much pain. His grief was like a tidal wave, tossing him in an emotional sea of sadness. He never lost sight of his faith. I'm not even sure if he ever faltered, but there was a piece of him that died with his son."

"I can't even imagine," April said, her eyes moist with emotion at the thought.

"Yeah." He agreed. "I was worried it would destroy him, put out his light for good. Maybe some part of me was selfish. I needed him and couldn't lose him, so I begged God to let me have it, asked him to lay the burden on my shoulders, and he did."

"What was it like?"

"Imagine it like emotional withdrawal. It came in waves, at times like taking a punch in the gut. We all experience loss, but to feel the loss of a parent's child is something else. There's a level of guilt that comes with it. There was no way Caleb could have prevented it. Alex was with a friend's family when they hit black ice and spun off the road. It's the type of accident that just happens, but there was still guilt, heavy guilt."

"How long did it last?"

"Several weeks, coming and going. Don't get me wrong. To this day, he still mourns the loss of his son. I was just able to carry the deep dark emotions that came with it."

"What was it like for him, did you ever ask?"

"Not right away. It felt self-serving and invasive to bring it up. I didn't even tell him about it until almost a year later. When it finally came up, Caleb described it as being able to breathe again after holding your breath under water for just a moment too long. He talked about an intense calm that settled into his spirit, a knowing that somehow things would be all right."

"What about you? During it?"

"It's hard to feel something you have no reason to feel. It messed with my brain a lot. With empathy, I could always feel bits and pieces. Sometimes more, sometimes less. With this, it wasn't just one piece. It was the entire range of emotions. It took a while, but through constant prayer and interaction with the Holy Spirit, I was able to sort it all out, and eventually, it faded."

"Would you change it? Taking from Caleb, or any of the others?"

"Not for all the money in the world. It helped my friend and many like him dealing with their demons, and it prepared me to deal with my own."

"Your own?" she asked, brows furrowed once again.

"Yes, we all have battles."

"What did it prepare you for?"

He glanced at his watch, avoiding her eyes. "That is a story that would take all night to tell. It's already starting to get dark, and we still have an hour long walk back to your car.

April sat in her car outside of Phil's, contemplating what she had learned about David and what she still didn't know. She felt no closer to finding out what all of this meant to her, but she was certain they would be seeing either other again soon. Even though it had only been a few minutes since he had given her his number, some Bible verses to look up, and a quick hug, she was eager for their next encounter, which they had planned for tomorrow afternoon.

A knock on her window startled her, causing her to jump back in her seat. Kyle D. stood on the other side of the window, with his silly grin and smoke slithering out from between his teeth. "Roll down your window," Kyle said through the glass, making the rolling motion with his hand. Hesitantly, she complied.

"Dude, where you been? I've been texting you for days and who was that big guy? Don't tell me he's a cop. You didn't go narc, did you? I'm pretty sure you have you tell me if you did. Are you wired? Can I see it?"

"Hi, Kyle, nice to see you too," she said, annoyed. "To answer your billion questions, I've been busy, back at my mom's. No, he's not a cop. No, I'm not a narc. I don't think I'd have to tell you if I was, and no, I'm not wearing a wire."

"Back at your mom's, eh? She still single? You know your mom's smoking hot right? I could literally be your step daddy."

"Ew, Kyle, don't be foul." She shuddered at the thought in disgust.

"So that guy, he's your boyfriend? Looks rich. Did April get herself a sugar daddy? Good thing you're not a narc, huh? People get weird about that shit. Disappearing for days, showing up with a freakin' behemoth. You sure he's not a cop? Did you even ask him? If he is, he's doing the wrong job. You know the Seahawks could use a mountain like that on their team. Come to think of it, he dresses too nice to be a cop. Bro's GQ, and I'm not even sure what that means. By the way, what happened to your face. Your eyes look bigger.

Her patience for his ramblings was running thin. *My god*, she thought. *Was I like this when I was high?* Knowing the paranoid and squirrel brain that came with using, she decided to ease his mind, despite her desire for a bath and the comfort of her bed. "My face?" she asked first.

"Yeah, man, all the black stuff, eyeliner I think. I'm not gay. I don't use the stuff, but Anthony and his band do when they perform. It's trippy man, like a freakin' movie, bro. You should see them getting ready. It's like whoa." He bounced from foot to foot, unable to stand still.

"I decided to change it up a bit," she replied, turning the heater up to combat the chilly air crawling through the open window.

"No, dude, you're still hot, just like younger looking, like look at me I go to college and have parents that love me." He laughed hysterically at his own joke, before his face tensed again with paranoia. "Seriously, bro, who's the guy? He's DEA, isn't he? I've heard they've been hanging around, busted a lab in Athol last week. Is he a cop? Like for real, don't screw with me, April."

"Kyle, I swear, he is not a cop," she answered, her mind reeling at the velocity of words spewing from his mouth on tobacco stained breath. "He's a friend from out of town. I actually met him at Phil's a few nights ago."

"Good, good. Okay. Cool. So yeah, I've been texting you for days. Got some new stuff, it's good too. Came from Portland. I got so much done, man, then slept for like, days, legit. So, you know it's good. This one's on me." He held up a small velvet pouch. "Just tell your friends. It'll be gone fast. Tell them to get while the getting's good."

"Sorry, Kyle, not this time. I'm at my mom's, and she'll kick me out." She felt a ping of guilt for lying, but how could she even begin to explain to a man so high he probably couldn't tie his shoes."

"No, bro, you going clean? Clean is the worst." He drew out the O.

"Something like that. Kyle, I gotta go. Mom's going to worry."

"You sure, man? Take it. On me, just in case. Just a little bit will ease the pain that's going to hit real soon."

She contemplated taking the bag. What it might feel like to just hold it, then thought about what David has said about choices and pushed those thoughts out of her mind. "Not this time," she said, rolling up the window. "See ya."

A few blocks later, she turned right on Division, leaving the broken-down buildings behind her, with the city lights shining ahead, when flashing blue and red lit up her rearview mirror. The familiar panic flooded her brain as she categorized the items in her car, out of habit. "Legal, legal, legal. Wait, I don't have anything. I'm not high. Oh, thank God." She rolled down her window as the officer neared her car.

"Good evening, miss, license and registration please."

She handed the officer her documents saying, "Sorry, sir, was I speeding? I thought it was thirty-five here."

"No, ma'am, just wanted to let you know you have a brake light out. Passenger side. Not going to ticket you for it tonight, just get it fixed. He handed her license and papers back. "Have a good one."

"Thank you, officer, you too."

She sat for a moment after he'd driven away, thinking of what might have happened if she had taken Kyle up on his offer. "Thank you, God," she whispered, pulling back into the street.

DAY 4

She had dreamt about him again, nearly the same as the night before. She still couldn't reconcile the man in her dream, David, with the man who had sat across from her at the coffee shop just yesterday. She thought of all the questions she could ask him to see if she could try to understand exactly what the dream meant, but it somehow felt intrusive just thinking about it.

Maye went back to work this morning, so at least she had the house to herself for a minute. She wasn't supposed to meet him until one, hours from now, and was anxiously trying to figure out what to do until then. She was surprised by how excited she was to see him again. Something about the way he spoke to her made her feel empowered, like she could take on the world.

For now, she would have to take on the house. Not that it was dirty, Maye just had a habit of living in constant chaos and clutter; something April couldn't stand. She started by doing the dishes and cleaning the kitchen. Feeling alone in the quiet of the house, she turned the radio on to a Christian station, K-LOVE, and continued her task. When the house was all but sparkling, she stood in front of her newly filled closet.

First, she tried on one of the flowing printed dresses Maye chose for her. Somehow, it made her feel like a kindergarten student. She stripped off the dress and decided on a pair of dark jeans with fashionably placed holes, a loose white tank top with lace lining, and a navy cardigan. Paired with a pair of wedge boots, she felt feminine and practical.

"What are you thinking?" she asked herself while applying light pink lipstick at the vanity. "No amount of makeup will ever make him interested in a girl like you." She wiped the lipstick away with a tissue and piled her hair on her head in a big messy bun. She finished just in time to leave for Phil's. She had offered to pick him up, but he declined preferring to walk.

She fought the urge to text him and cancel. The whole drive to Phil's all she could think about were the movies where the most popular guy asks the most unpopular girl to prom, then either ditched or found some terrible way to embarrass her in front of everybody. April was the unpopular girl, and David was the jock. She felt like she was walking into a trap. How could a guy like that even give her the time of day? He was probably just pitying her. It was the "Christian" thing to do after all.

He hadn't stopped thinking about her since they had parted ways the night before. It had been a long time since he had been able to laugh so freely. He was amazed by how easily she laughed and even more so by how her laugh appealed to him. Thinking about it, his heart nearly skipped a beat when he saw her car pull into an empty space in front of Phil's.

"Hey, girl," he said, refraining again from hugging her. "What do you want to do?"

She shrugged awkwardly, seeming somewhat withdrawn.

"Well, we could walk? Where's your favorite place to go?"

A small grin lit up her face. "I haven't been for years, but we could go out to the Post Falls dam. I used to go all the time with my dad when I was a kid. There are some great trails, but we're not walking there."

"Sure, let's go!"

The drive was about forty minutes, spent mostly with him trying to pull anything out of her. He couldn't figure out what, but something was plaguing her. Finally, he gave up on small talk and turned the radio up, singing along with his favorite songs.

She pulled into a small parking lot, with a large sign welcoming them to Q'emiln Park. He could see immediately why she liked the area. The air was fresh and the landscape incredible.

"Lead the way," he said, when they had exited her car. They walked the first several minutes in silence, until finally reaching the dam, which was opened. The thunder of water passing under them was awe inspiring. He looked over rails and couldn't help but think of how oddly inviting the swirling water looked, as it kicked up a fine mist. He looked toward April and smiled. Her eyes were closed, and she looked completely at peace. He again fought the urge to pull her into him, asking instead, "So, you said your dad brought you here, do you still see him often?"

Her face stiffened. "No, not really. He got remarried a few years back. I haven't seen him much since."

"Really? How come?"

"Well, Susan's nice and all, she just has two teenage girls. I guess they were preteens back then, and you know, heroin addicts aren't exactly the best role model to have around. I think she tried to take me under her wing but eventually gave up. I don't blame her."

"So, you just stayed with your mom?"

"That's hard to answer. I guess yes. At first, I stayed with her. After he left her, she couldn't quite figure out how to adult anymore. Or maybe she adulted a little too well. Who knows. In any case, her habits became more important to her than taking care of me. I think I was fourteen when he left her, I stayed until I was sixteen. At some point, I just got sick of being the parent and left."

"What do you mean?"

"Mom's a free spirit. She's always been. I think Dad calmed that side of her. At least for a while. Without him, she lost it. I mean, she started drinking and taking pills before he ever left. That's what ultimately drove him out the door. Without him, she was basically free to do whatever she pleased without any sort of accountability. And she did."

"That sounds terrible. Is that why you left?"

"Part of it. I think more than that was her hypocrisy and constant manipulation. I was a straight A student, a pretty good kid actually. I got busted one time for drinking wine coolers with friends, and she lost it. Not like, normal parent, don't drink, make smart choices, blah blah. No, she went nuts. Basically, accused me of being an alcoholic and said I belonged with him. She said it with such contempt. I know I'm more like him than like her; at least, in some ways, but the way she said it made me feel like I had done something so wrong. Like my existence and similarities to him were a burden for her, so I left. It seems weird to say, but I felt like an orphan, or maybe wished I was one. Dad tried to see me, but Mom fought hard to keep him away, and then when I started using at eighteen, he wasn't really 'allowed' to have me around, and I don't think my mom really cared if I was there or not. I just did my own thing."

"I can't imagine. What was it like?"

"Which part?"

"Moving out so young, being on your own."

"We really don't have to talk about that. Think of any movie with a drug addict. Boom, you now know my life."

"You said you started using at eighteen, what made you start?"

She started to answer, then paused as an inky black crow began to caw above their heads pulling her eyes to the sky. She watched it fly higher into the sky as if watching the moment her own innocence slipped away. "I needed to stop being me. Or at least stop feeling like the me that I was wasn't enough. I think." She paused again, looking for words. "I think I thought back then that if I could just forget about it all, I would be okay. But…can we not talk about this? Like I said, you can watch a movie and get the gist. I was nothing special, just your typical druggie."

Although tempted to push, he decided instead to move on. "Okay, fair enough. Then change of subject, what are you dreams, your goals?"

She hesitated before responding, returning her eyes to the churning water below. "I don't know."

"Nothing?"

"I never thought I'd make it this long. I've seen so many people die, either overdose or some stupid accident while they were high. I just assumed that would be me. People like that don't have dreams."

"What about now?"

"I don't know."

"But that's not you anymore. You can dream big and accomplish anything."

She looked back to him, sadness in her eyes. "What is there for someone like me? I'm a high school dropout. I have no education, no job experience, nothing. I'm not exactly the type of person who can just go out and conquer the world."

"That's an excuse, and you know it. You're bright, beautiful, uncannily charming, and can do anything you want."

She blushed at the compliment. "That's nice of you to say, but I don't know that it's true."

"It's the exact truth! If you could do anything, anything at all, what would it be?"

She paused for a moment, considering her answer, "I think. Well, I think I'd want to find a way to help people like me. People are so quick to decide what we are and deem us unworthy, and maybe we are, but sometimes I think if anybody would have taken the time to look and really see me, I may have wanted to change. People always say they see you, but they don't. Even at the rehab clinic I went to once or twice, it's like the nurses were so used to seeing people back again and again that they nodded and smiled through plastic faces when you talked about getting clean. They never asked about dreams. They never talked about anything relevant. I think the whole 'one day at a time' thing is garbage. Trust me, I get it. The addiction and escaping it *is* one day at a time, but it's so focused on the now. Like, all I could think about was not using, because all I was doing was not using. It seems so petty a thing to say, but how great would it be if someone had asked me 'Okay, what's next?' It wasn't like that. It was, 'Okay, so next don't use.'"

"I think you'd be amazing as one of those nurses. You can be the one who asks the right questions from experience."

"I kind of cheated." She laughed.

"I wouldn't call it that, you just had a little extra help."

They hiked through the hills until the sun started its decent. Sitting on her car, they watched it fall below the horizon.

"I'm starving," she said.

"Should we hit up Phil's? That club sandwich was something to brag about. I could go for another."

The drive back, she was livelier. He wasn't sure what it was, maybe the cool river mist blowing in her face, maybe realizing that she had a chance at dreams, or maybe just walking had the same effect on her as it did on him. He wasn't sure, but he loved it. She smiled and laughed, singing along to the songs that played and pointed out some of the area's history.

Once at Phil's, they talked more, laughing and choosing songs on the jukebox. Every moment he spent with her, he was more and more drawn to her. He tried but couldn't fathom how he had managed to live before knowing her.

At one point, she had asked him about Jesus, wanting to know more about the man she had read about.

"What is it you want to know?"

"You really believe everything the Bible says about him?"

"Every word of it."

"How?"

"How do I believe it? I don't know. I guess at some point, I recognized it as truth, somewhere deep inside me and have never lost that. It's not always easy. Well, let me take that back. Believing in him is easy. Living by his word, not so much. I think there's this idea that people have. They think that once they accept him as their savior, everything gets better. When things don't get better, they stop trying to live like him. I've found that things don't necessarily get better. You're still in the same world. Still subject to the same people and the same pain. The difference is having peace that surpasses whatever situation you're in."

"What do you mean accept him?"

"The Bible says, 'If you confess that Jesus is the Lord and believe that God raised him from death, you will be saved. For it is by our faith that we are put right with God. It is by our confessions that we are saved.'"

"I don't get it. I've always believed there was some higher power, but I don't think I ever really paid much attention to Jesus. What does he have to do with any of it?"

He smiled. This was his favorite discussion to have with people. "Basically, sin created a wall of sorts between God and man. Back in the Old Testament, God's people sacrificed animals to make right with God. Those sacrifices were accepted as penance for their sins."

"That seems brutal."

"It probably was. In Eden, when the first sin was committed, God slaughtered an animal to make covering for Adam and Eve. Some theologians believe that this act showed how innocence was used to cover up man's sin. Essentially, people were paying for their sins with the blood of the innocent animal. That leads directly into who Jesus was. He is called the Lamb of God. If you haven't yet, read more in the Gospels—Mathew, Mark, Luke, and John. They talk a lot about the life Christ lived, along with his death. When he was hung on the cross, or sacrificed, his blood covered sin. It made us pure again. He is now our advocate."

"Advocate?"

"God can't look upon sin. Jesus is our man in the middle. When we sin and subsequently ask for forgiveness, he covers that. Because he intervenes, we are able to have a relationship with the Father."

"What does it mean to ask for forgiveness?"

"To repent. To acknowledge your sin and turn from it."

"What happens if you do it again?"

"Jesus covers that too. It says in John that if we confess our sins, God is faithful and just to forgive us our sins and cleanse us from all unrighteousness."

"So, I can just go around sinning and expect forgiveness?"

"I won't say that forgiveness is conditional. It's not. When you've accepted Christ as Lord, you enter into a sort of covenant with him. Your life no longer becomes about yourself. You start to live in a way that is pleasing to God. That doesn't mean you don't sin, you do, I do, but somewhere within you, God begins to change you. If you truly believe, then you understand when you do wrong and understand why it was wrong. So, while you may sin the same way more than once, through relationship with God, that changes. The greatest desire of my heart is to live like Jesus. Of course, I fall short, but every time, I turn from that. Learn from the mistakes and become better for the grace of God."

"When I accept him, am I just held to new rules?"

"Not anymore so than an infant is."

"What an odd response."

"It's true. One of the biggest lies the devil tells is that people aren't enough. When a new believer sins, he lays that guilt on thick. Condemns them in that. Would you condemn a baby for head butting? No. You might scold it, if it were intentional, but you can't hold your knowledge of right and wrong against the child. When you become a believer, you are reborn. I think a lot of people expect that they are reborn as this fully matured believer. They aren't. Each day, you grow a little bit more, learn a little bit more, act a little bit different. There is amazing power in that growth. I only wish people would recognize that it does take time."

"Am, am I a new believer?"

He smiled in her direction. "I don't know, April. Are you?"

Back at the hotel, David twisted and turned on the bed. His mind was moving a thousand thoughts per second, and he was unable to focus on any one. A picture of April's emerald eyes, followed by memories of the first time he walked out of Kansas City on a mission, then a flash of Hope's face, smiling happy, singing songs of worship; a moment so close and yet so far away.

The next memory nearly flung him to his feet. It was the last memory he had of his sister. He had watched as she threw a glass of water at her reflection, shattering the mirror displaying it. Her eyes were hollow, hair unkempt, and sweatpants stained with what looked like mustard. She had just broken up with her boyfriend, one of David's good friends, without cause and was now fuming with anger toward David and the world. Hope had always had a flare for drama, so he left. He didn't know.

Now on his feet, David slipped back into his jeans and pulled the sweater over his head. If he wasn't going to get any sleep, he could at least walk. He left the hotel room, playing Modern Post on his phone. Once on the street, he immediately began to feel better, and he deeply inhaled the brisk fall air.

He walked. Aimlessly putting foot to pavement, he moved forward. No awareness of the bodies lingering in alleyways, fearing he was DEA, or the homeless squatting in empty shops, liquor thick on their breath. He just walked.

At a cross street, he suddenly felt the familiar pull of the compass. Left, down four blocks, left, right forward, forward, forward. He began to recognize the area (you might call it his new hangout spot); left, forward, forward, right, Phil's.

David felt dread begin to climb in his chest for April. Had she caved? Was she back at Phil's for more tequila and whiskey? What would she think if she saw him here? That he was some crazy stalker keeping tabs on her every move? His panic spread out to his limbs, arms shaking and feet now unwilling to press forward. His mind now covered in what felt like a blanket of soot. He was only able to mumble, "God."

After several minutes and several looks from curious patrons entering the bar (apparently eleven on Friday night was the busy time), he finally willed himself through the door. The place was packed, a far different crowd than the ones here at one Tuesday morning, all dressed like April had been. Black hair, black skinny jeans with holes in the knees, and most of them wearing some variation of black band shirt. He wondered how many of them she might know. He scanned the room looking for her face, then surrendered to the arrow that pulled him toward the bar.

To his surprise, Bee was behind the counter, along with a bleached hair skeletal-looking man who couldn't have been older than thirty. Bee's face lit up when she saw him. "Well, I'll be damned," she said, placing the now expected, little square napkin in front of him. "I wasn't expecting to see you back here again. What'll it be?"

"I'll be honest, Bee. I wasn't expecting to see you here either. Any chance you have coffee ready?"

"Split shift, baby. Friday night's the money-making night. I sure don't have any coffee, but I can start a pot special just for you. This group's more of the whiskey type than coffee. I imagine it makes them feel cool, like Johnny Cash. Wannabee's, the lot of them." She shook her head in disgust, calling out. "Bones, cover the bar. I'll be back in a minute." The skeletal man, Bones, nodded without looking up from the cocktail he was making, as Bee disappeared behind black swinging doors.

David scanned the room again, this time looking closely at each of the dark-haired women, hoping to see April's face, while also desperately wishing that she not be among the crowd. He didn't want to consider what it might mean if she was. Mostly happy but a little disappointed not to see her, he turned back to the bar and again felt the arrow pointing toward the black doors Bee had gone through just moments before. He wondered what it was she might be battling—physical or emotional pains?

He suddenly noticed a short, stocky, bearded man near the doors. He had a sort of haunted look on his face, with thick purple bags under his eyes. Like he hadn't slept in years. The look wasn't what caught David's attention. He was fairly used to the different forms bondage takes, more so he was caught off guard by a sense that he knew the man, like he'd met him before, but was unable to place it. The odds of him knowing someone in Spokane were relatively slim.

The bearded man looked up and caught David's gaze. His eyes so familiar they brought an odd feeling of rage to David's gut. He quickly turned away, focusing instead on Bee, exiting the swinging doors with a steaming mug of black coffee. "Here you go, sug. Flag me down if you need anything more."

He sat at the bar for another two hours, sipping his coffee slowly and looking at the door expectantly every time it opened, hoping it wouldn't be her. When the stocky man left, David felt a pull to go after him, instead staying at the bar, chalking it up to the same irrational feelings he had earlier when he first spotted the man.

By one fifteen in the morning, Phil's was mostly empty. The Bone man began closing tasks, wiping down tables, as Bee came to him, leaning on the bar. "One more for you?"

"No, no, I'm fine. Thank you."

"I'll be honest. I've been fighting this urge all night, but I'm just so tickled I can't hold it in anymore," she stated, wiping the counter between them. "Did April find you? She came in looking for you yesterday."

He laughed joyfully at her question. "She sure did, Miss Bee."

"Oh good, you two are just so perfect for each other. I think you're good for her, much better than these skinny stoner kids she spends time with. Take her away from this hellhole, David. It's a trap."

He felt his face flush, stammering, "No, no, it's not like that."

"Sure, tell that to your beat red face and cat caught tongue. You like her." She smiled deviously.

"Enough about me," he spit out. "Tell me about you, Bee. What's got you down?"

"Kid, I'm fifty-two years old, work at a dying bar, haven't talked to my kids in years, have a dog so old it craps wherever it feels like, and have carpal tunnel so bad in my right wrist, they tell me I need surgery. Oh, and did I mention, good ol' Phil here doesn't offer health coverage. So, I think the real question is, what's right with me?"

"Well, you've got a beautiful smile and a spirit so bright it casts an amazing comfort, like the sun's ray, on anybody around you, just to start. May I pray for your wrist?" He put his hand out on the counter, palm up. She slowly, tentatively, placed hers on top of it. Covering her hand with his other, he said, "Praise the Lord, my soul, all my inmost being, praise his holy name. Praise the Lord my soul and forget not all his benefits. Who forgives all your sins and heals your diseases, who redeems your life from the pit and crowns you with love and compassion, who satisfies desires with good things, so that youth is renewed like the eagles. Amen."

"Amen," she whispered. "Nobody's ever prayed for me before."

"Well, I have and now I'll never stop." He patted her hand once more, saying, "Bless you." Before leaving, a dull ache forming in his wrists.

When she got home, April planted herself at the kitchen table with a notebook and the Bible app on her phone. David had given her a reading assignment. He had said that to truly understand him, April will have to start understanding more about God, specifically about Jesus. "Do I have to go to church?" April had asked when they reached her car.

"Not necessarily," he had answered with easy grin. "At least, not yet. But relationship is very important as you start to build your faith and understand God's purpose for you."

She was still dubious that the creator of the entire universe would have a purpose for her but didn't feel like getting into that conversation with him. "What about you?" she had asked instead. "You spend most of your time alone, don't you?"

"Some of us are still wandering in the wilderness."

What does that even mean?"

"You'll figure it out when you read about Moses. Good night, April." He had again disappeared into the night as she watched. She thought back to when he had hugged her, part of her longing to feel that closeness again. He had felt so safe. A feeling that faded away quickly when she realized she was alone in the street in front of Phil's. *How quickly things change*, she thought, trying to redirect her focus to the app open on her phone. Selecting the book of Matthew, her mind wandered again. This time, to Kyle's unexpected appearance last night, and how different the two men were. Both equally important to her life, Kyle representing her past, chaos, and an unbridled need to forget who she was, and David a persistent calm, yet mysterious force pointing her toward her future. Quite literally if you considered his compass.

She wondered, the unread pages of Matthew displayed on her screen, what it was he was avoiding? Not that she had ever been one to give credence to her dreams, but there was something happening that she couldn't quite figure out. She thought of the verse she had read before finding him in the laundromat, which had filled her with an odd sense of anticipation.

"God"—she prayed out loud—"I don't know who you are, but I'm ready to learn, and I believe that you are moving, not just in my life, but in David's too. Somehow, you brought him to me and now I need him to learn more about you and to learn more about me. Please help keep him safe. Protect him, God. Whatever it is that's coming, guard him."

A rustling in the doorway drew her eyes open. Maye stood, with a guilty look, just out of the reach of the kitchen light.

"Hi, Mom."

"Sorry to interrupt," Maye said sheepishly, stepping over the threshold into the kitchen. "I heard you talking, so I thought maybe somebody was here."

"Nope, just me."

"What are you doing." Maye slipped into a chair.

"Praying I think. I was going to read, but I got distracted."

"Praying? To God?"

"Yes."

"About David?"

"Yes."

"Why? Shouldn't you pray for yourself? It seems like this David guy has it figured out."

April squirmed uncomfortable in her chair. She wasn't sure exactly what to say so she chose honesty. "I'm not sure, Mom, something just feels off."

"About him? Is this that fifty shades thing again? Is he actually some sort of freak?"

April sighed, annoyed by her mother's apparent hopes that the man who had saved her was deranged. "No, Mom. Not about him, around him almost."

"You're not even making sense, April," her mother stated, leaving the chair to pour herself a glass of wine from the box on the counter.

April considered chastising her, instead deciding to tell of the dream. "I've been dreaming about him."

"Oh?" Maye's interests were piqued, and she returned to the table.

This time, April's sigh was audible. "Not like that, Mother."

"Then like what?"

April told of her dreams, how they had started as a replay of the night she had first met David. Vivid memories that were comforting, almost affirmation that she hadn't gone crazy but then, a few nights later, how she had dreamt of him trapped inside a coffin, like a box covered in a large chain. "The look on his face, Mom. I can't explain it. It's like despair with a deep sorrow rooted in his eyes. In some weird way, it makes me think of the crazed needy look junkies get when they've gone too long without whatever vice sustains them. I just can't shake this feeling that something is about to happen."

"That sounds ominous," Maye said, pondering the hidden meaning of April's dream.

"I know. I think maybe somehow he needs me right now as much as I need him."

Maye nodded in agreement, earlier traces of doubt no longer written on her face. She stood. "Well, maybe tonight you'll figure it out. I'm going to bed, back to work in the morning. Good night."

"Good night, Mom."

As she walked toward the hall, Maye paused. "April, will you pray for me, too?"

The street was empty when he left Phil's. Whatever crowd occupied Friday night had dissipated, leaving behind only the cool fall air and an assortment of cigarette butts on the curb. He thought about going back to the hotel for sleep, but some distant memory plagued his mind, causing an uncomfortable feeling of discontent. For a moment, the ghostly thought had glided forward, teasing him with the possibility of remembrance, but like a shadow, it scurried away when he attempted to grasp it.

So, he walked. The night was cool but not yet cold. Leaves sang their restless song as they clamored to remain fully attached to the branches, which gave them life. It was a feeling he could relate to. Despite his wandering ways, he was and had always been a creature of habit and solitude. The events of the past few days left him shaken, unable to find solid footing and for the first time in years, questioning his decisions. He wanted to call Caleb, and he knew if he did, Caleb would answer, but what would he even say? "Something doesn't seem right?" What? What didn't seem right? He couldn't place it and couldn't willingly wake up his friend without a valid reason, so he walked.

He walked by empty storefronts, broken down buildings, and a few fluorescent lights without their normal blue glow. He walked without his usual scripture or hymn. Unlit the streets became unfamiliar. His mind was preoccupied and yet unable to remain on one subject. He was unfocused. The feeling that was eluding him, weighing heavily on his shoulders. He tried to turn his mind to the Psalms but found himself unable to conjure the words that had so frequently brought him comfort, instead thinking of April.

He thought of how badly he wanted to protect her. How worried he was that she was just an innocent lamb in the midst of jackals, and he worried that something was coming and he wouldn't be able to save her. He thought of Hope.

Hope was always so full of joy and life and love, until one day, she just wasn't. If he had only known the truth, he could have been there for her, but they didn't tell him. He hadn't found out until two weeks after her funeral. He was at his parent's house when the detective in charge of her case showed up. In that moment, he not only learned of his sister's assault, he also learned of his parent's betrayal. Later, they had told him that Hope insisted he never know, but in that moment, he saw only their deception.

He had been staying with them since her death, overwhelmed with emotions he had needed their odd detachment to stay grounded, but the unexpected knock at the door changed everything.

Detective Sanchez was pleasant enough, but David sensed immediately the wiry man's desire to leave. He had sat in the living room chair, rigid, declining an offer of coffee made by David's mother. They all sat; David and his mother on the overstuffed couch opposite the detective and David's father.

"We believe we've found Hope's assailant." The detective started, causing David to search his mother's face for an explanation as Sanchez continued, "The man who attacked your daughter was admitted to Saint Luke's Hospital about twelve days ago due to an overdose. He had a warrant out for his arrest on similar charges, and we were able to get DNA. His DNA matches the rape kit done on Hope the night of her assault. He's out of critical condition now, and the city prosecutor is pressing charges." He continued by telling the three of what to expect in the upcoming months, asked them to be ready to receive calls from the prosecutor and potentially additional detectives. He then thanked them for their time and left, with a copy of details he was permitted to share on Hope's case in a manila folder on the coffee table.

After Detective Sanchez left, David stared at his parents. He tried to find the words to ask for the truth, begged in his own mind, but he couldn't stand to hear it, and he left.

That night, he walked away and he hadn't stopped walking since. Returning home only for holidays and the anniversary of his sister's funeral. He hadn't gone back for the court proceedings, unable to face his sister's attacker, but Caleb had sent him the file, all of it, including details of the man's plea deal. Over the years, he had read bits and pieces of the file, often forced to stop at the sheer brutality of what his sister faced.

And now, with those memories trailing, tonight he walked.

DAY 5

The next morning, she felt refreshed. She had dreamt of him again but didn't feel the same anxiety as she had before. She was confident the dream had some unknown meaning, and she was determined to find out what it was. With a glass of orange juice in front of her at the kitchen table, she opened up her messaging app and typed, "David, need to talk, meet for lunch?"

After half an hour with no response, she assumed he was still sleeping and tried to figure out what to do with herself. Maye was at work, and April had the house to herself. After cleaning up the breakfast dishes, she decided to sit outside with the worn Bible she had found on an old bookshelf. She grabbed a notebook, pen, her phone and the Bible and made herself comfortable at the small patio table.

She thought about reading more of the New Testament but decided instead to see if the hefty book could provide insight into her dreams or the meaning of the chains. She opened Google on her phone and typed in "Bible verses about dreams." Unsure of what to expect, she chose the first website returned. Wading through page after page of dream-related verses, while interesting, did not bring her any closer to understanding her own dream, although she was now convinced that God was trying to communicate with her. It seemed dreams were often used to tell of future comings. She even made a note to learn more about Joseph and Daniel, two dreamers mentioned frequently in the webpages she searched. Without an understanding of what her dreams meant, she decided to change tactics and see if she could find anything on the meaning of the chains.

Before returning to Google, she checked her messages, nothing new, and the time, almost eleven. It had been two hours since she had texted him. She was tempted to send another message, but decided that if she didn't hear from him by noon, she would call and invite him to lunch. Feeling slightly annoyed by his lack of response, she returned to her search. Starting first in Psalm 107 and then to Romans. The first verses, Psalm 107:14–16 read, "He brought them out of darkness and broke away their chains. Let them give thanks to the Lord for his unfailing love and his wonderful deeds for mankind. For he breaks down gates of bronze and cuts through bars of iron."

Interesting, but she wasn't entirely sure what it meant. Next on to Romans 8:15, "The Spirit you received does not make you slaves, so that you live in fear again; rather, the Spirit you received brought about your adoption to sonship. And by him we cry, 'Abba, Father.'"

She sat in the shade, pondering what she had read. While still not entirely sure what this all meant, there were two things she now knew without a doubt. First, her dream meant *something*, and second, whatever chain David was wearing, only God could break it. A small voice in her head whispered that she would be the conduit God would use for the job. She checked her phone again, nothing.

She couldn't help him if he wouldn't open up to her. The display read 12:13, so she dialed his number and listed to the rings, growing increasingly concerned with each one unanswered. "Call me," she said at the beep.

She tried to read more but couldn't focus. The words jumbled up into tiny piles of lines as she stared at them. The feeling of unworthiness had started to float around her once again. She thought they had a great time together yesterday but was apparently mistaken. Several hours later, hours spent trapped in self-pity and boredom, her feelings of doubt began to subside. Replaced with worry and fear for David. No matter how hard she tried, she couldn't believe that he would just leave without a word.

He sat in the hotel room with the shades drawn and the light off. Unable to make sense of the previous night. He tried to recite the verses, read from Psalm, and listen to his favorite songs, but none of it brought him the peace he was desperate for. His mind kept repeating the events of the night before.

His walking had brought him to a run-down apartment complex. It wasn't until he had reached the parking lot that he realized he had been drawn here by the compass. Wandering between the buildings, he found a small park, dimly lit by one old lamp. He scanned the shadows. Once confident he was the only living thing in the park, he stood still, waiting on the pull to give him direction. After a few minutes of nothing, he climbed the small playset and settled into the damp wood, waiting for his next move. It wasn't until he sat that he realized the burning in his legs. His watch showed almost 4:00 a.m. He had been walking for nearly three hours and had no idea where he was.

His eyes were suddenly heavy, tempted to surrender to sleep. Just as he was about to climb down and continue back to the hotel, a shadow emerged from the darkness at the opposite side of the park. David had watched as the man moved from the shadows to a bench near the light. In that moment, he had felt the tickling of remembrance playing once more with his mind. The man was short and stocky with dark stubble covering the lower half of his face. David had watched the man light a cigarette, throw it down angrily, and immediately light another. It was the man from the bar.

David suddenly felt his fingers clenching into fists and an unexplainable rage burned within him as he watched the man. After finishing his cigarette, the man stood, looked around, threw his hands up, and returned to the bench. This time, he had planted his face in his palms and wailed. The animal-like noise was unlike anything David had ever heard, and it didn't stop. He had sat and watched as the man cried, tears streaming from his face. The man began beating his own head. David felt the pull of compass so strong he could almost see it, but he didn't move. He told himself it was too dangerous to approach the distressed man, but he knew that was a lie. He had faced more dangerous situations than this without batting an eye.

The truth was, he didn't want to. For the first time since Caleb, he could not choose to help the crying man. Instead, he had spent the next forty-five minutes listening without feeling an ounce of care. He felt nothing as his heart hardened in his chest, unsure of why he felt such disdain toward this unknown man. He had then spent nearly four hours finding his way back to the hotel where he had sat awake since.

He had seen April's first text come through but couldn't find the emotional capacity to respond. Instead, he reached for the hotel's Bible and began reading in first Samuel. He read with the detached mechanical focus he had as a child.

Later that night, April tossed and turned in her sheets, unable to calm her mind and grasp onto sleep, which felt so close and yet just out of reach. Anxiously, she grabbed her phone from the bedside table, blinking at the bright like that displayed 11:15 p.m.

She felt a desperate need to see him, to make sure he was safe. Not from the monsters of this world but from the demons who played in the shadows of the mind. She thought of the moment just days before when she had been gripped by lies, and she wondered if the chain she had seen over David in her dream was representative of a lie he had been unable to shake.

Frustrated, she slipped on the bedside lamp and freed herself from the tangled linens. There was a time when a few shots of whiskey and a couple of sleeping pills would have called her name, and she would have gladly answered, following them to complete mental oblivion, but now she shook her head in disgust at the thought.

She paced in the small room trying to make sense of the week. Up until yesterday, he had seemed happy to be around her. Maybe she had been delusional to think there was something else there, especially with her past, but she couldn't believe he had just decided to be done with her. He had promised to tell her everything, and she couldn't make herself believe that he would break that promise.

She felt lies begin to form in her mind, familiar feelings of being used and dumped, the desperate longing to be desired and loved, overshadowed by shame and never being enough. She sat heavily on her bed, opening her messages, fighting the urge to text him again. She had tried almost every two hours without a response. She felt angry and foolish, trapped in a cycle in her mind. She was torn between past experiences and coming to terms with David's seeming rejection. She closed out of the app and opened the Bible on her phone, turning again to Psalm 107, reading again the verses that had brought her comfort throughout the day.

After reading through the verses several times, her anger had subsided. She threw her phone down on the bed and began pacing again. Maybe he had been pulled away by the compass. He mentioned that he didn't stay in most places for very long. He was always on the move. She could kick herself for not asking what hotel he was at (it seemed somehow improper at the time), but if she knew the hotel, she could at least call and see if he had checked out.

Instead of killing herself trying to figure out what happened, she decided to go to Phil's. Bee should be working and maybe she would know something. She quickly pulled on her jeans, left her face bare, and silently slipped out the front door.

The drive was quick but filled with worry. Even though it was nearing one, some of the old crowd might still be there. She couldn't muster up the strength to deal with the mocking that was bound to come or make up excuses for her sudden absence. To her delight, the street out front was mostly void of cars. The ones still parked in the street were unfamiliar to her.

The bar matched the street, a few grizzly men at the pool table, one banging the old jukebox, some middle-aged women at a corner cackling, and a bearded man sitting at the end of the bar with a morose look on his face and an empty drink sitting in front of him. As April approached the bar, the bearded man waved down Bones for another drink.

"One sec, A," Bones said, pouring a stiff Jim Beam for the bearded man. Bones had always had a weird way of shortening words and names so he spoke as infrequently as possible, an odd trait for a bartender. At one point, he had began calling her Ape, but luckily, he finally landed on A. Walking toward her, he asked, "The use?"

"No, not tonight. Maybe just coffee."

"K."

As he started to walk toward the back, April called out, "Wait. Where's Bee? Shouldn't she be on tonight?"

Bones shrugged. "Said some guy changed her life. She's going home." He walked away.

"Some guy" might be David, who else would show up in a place like this and inspire a woman to make peace with her family after so many years to drive across two states home to them? "A man like David," she said out loud, quickly covering her mouth with her hand.

"Huh?" the bearded man grunted in her direction.

"Sorry." April felt a flush rise to her face. "I didn't mean to say what I was thinking. I don't think I've seen you around before, are you new to the area?"

"Kind of, a few months I guess."

"Oh, where from?"

"Missouri."

"Well, welcome. I'm April."

"Stephen." The man nodded and returned to his drink, as Bones came out with her coffee. She thought about asking him more about himself, but he seemed about as talkative as Bones, so she turned her attention to the two women laughing loudly in the corner; their intoxication somehow magnifying her own sobriety. They seemed to have struck up a conversation with the pool players, who had abandoned their game in favor of a chance to flirt.

She listened as one of the men offered a drink to the giggling woman who quickly accepted and watched as the two made their way to a darker corner of the bar, leaving their friends sitting uncomfortably in silence. Despite her curiosity, she had to look away when the interaction became PG-13, in fear the rating might go up quickly. As Bones brought her another steaming cup of coffee, the pair exited the bar, leaving the other two behind.

"That didn't take much," the bearded man said from his perch.

"It didn't take much at all." She agreed, her mind filling with shame at the judgment. How many times had she left Phil's so willingly? Her phone vibrated on the bar in front of her, a new text message. "Meet me at the wagon at Riverfront if you're awake."

He had tried to sleep, guiltily ignoring April's persistent texts, but found himself trapped in a TV guide channel loop of memories. Flashing images of his last encounter with Hope, the subsequent fight with his parents, and again in the park with the crying man he couldn't bring himself to approach. His worst moments danced through his mind like a soap opera.

After finally relenting that sleep wasn't in his future, he had spent the next several hours reading the hotel Bible without epiphany, finding instead a postcard of the Big Red Wagon tucked in its pages. Despite his physical and emotional exhaustion, he decided again to walk. This time with a destination, to Riverfront Park and the wagon, hoping to find clarity on the way. He didn't find what he was searching for, but the crisp air and long walk did help fight back visions that plagued him.

Now, David sat on a bench near the wagon, a staple of the area. During the day, it was occupied by screaming kids bundled in warm fall clothes, but now, it sat ominously empty, reflecting only the headlights of the occasionally passing car.

When he had texted her, he tried to tell himself he was doing it for her, but at his core, he knew that he needed to see her. He needed to be with someone who *saw* him. He felt a flutter in his stomach when he saw a small form walking intently toward the bench.

"What happened?" she demanded, the fire he had been so drawn to flickering fiercely in her eyes. "I thought you'd just left, without so much as a good-bye." He stood, pulling her in close, holding her tightly until he felt the tenseness in her shoulders give, and she wrapped her arms around him. "I thought you'd left me," she whispered, this time into his jacket.

"I'd never leave you. Let's walk." He pulled away. She nodded, wiping her hands across her eyes. They walked in silence for a moment, before he asked, "Why did you believe me?"

"Huh?" She looked up at him, a look of confusion forming on her brows.

"When I told you what I do, why did you believe me? Some guy walks up to you on an empty street in the middle of the night, tells you he can take your pain, and you just go with it?"

"Oh. I guess I felt like I didn't have a choice. Besides, what did I have to lose? I was renting a room that couldn't pass for a closet, living on alcohol, almost any drug I could scrounge up money for, and french fries, and hadn't kept the same job for more than a handful of weeks. What did I have to lose? And I guess, somehow, I trusted you. I've always been able to read people, although I clearly never listened to my gut." She giggled. "Anyway, taking you to Phil's felt like a safe way to learn more. Then, when you offered to do what you do, what crazy addict would turn that down? I never wanted to need the stuff. At some point, it goes from being fun to being a spider bite that constantly itches, and all you can do to stop the itch is give in." She paused, looking up at him. "Who wouldn't want a chance to be rid of that?"

"I see."

"Why do you ask? It seems an odd question after so many years of doing what you do."

"I think I messed it up."

"What?"

"This thing, this gift. There's always been an agreement. God leads and I follow. Well, last night, I didn't follow."

"Let's go up," she said, motioning to the metal stairs leading into the belly of the wagon. "Then you can tell me."

When they were as comfortable as possible on the cold wagon floor, David continued. "Last night, or I guess now, it was the night before. After I left you at your car, I was worried about you so I went back to Phil's just to see if you were there. I waited around for a while, but the place emptied out. I had a feeling there was someone I was supposed to help, but it wasn't focused, so I prayed for Bee and then I left. But my mind was uneasy, like I'd missed something, so I decided to walk. He told her of the encounter with the crying man. "I just watched, April. For the first time since all this started with Caleb, I ignored the call. Not so much ignoring as outright disobeying, and I don't know what that means. I haven't felt him since that night. No songs or verses have stirred his peace in me. I've been alone and empty."

He watched as April thought about what he had shared. "We have to find him," she finally stated.

He stood suddenly, exacerbated by the situation and needing to move. "How, April? How? I told you, I don't have the connection right now. The Wi-Fi has been turned off."

"Well, I don't have the compass thing, and I found you at the laundromat."

David pondered her statement. "How?"

"I prayed for God to help me find you then just walked and I did. So, maybe if we pray about this, God can guide us without the whole compass thing."

"April," he paused. "I don't pray."

Her eyebrows shot up, "Of course, you do. I've seen you."

"No, I mean I don't pray my own words. I pray biblical verses as they apply to situations. I haven't prayed a unique prayer since." He stopped, leaning over the side of the wagon.

"Since?" she prodded, scrambling to her feet. "Since what, David?"

He sighed heavily. "Since Hope died."

"Hope? Who is Hope?"

"Hope is, was my sister. She died almost seven years ago." Then with a sudden realization, he added, "Seven years ago tomorrow."

She was speechless, stumbling to find the right response. "I…I am so sorry. Oh my god, I am so sorry."

He could feel her heart aching for him, could see the look of dismay in her eyes, so different than the pity he was so accustomed to back at home. She turned her head from him, leaning over the side of the wagon. "April." He reached out and touched her arm. She turned to him, wet trails on her face.

"I'm so sorry, David. I can't imagine the grief you've been carrying." This time, she wrapped her arms around him.

For the first time since his sister's death, he wept into April's shoulder.

When the sobs that wracked his body finally subsided, she released him saying, "Don't go back to the hotel. You can stay with me."

He laughed, pulling away from her with raised eyebrows.

"Not like that." She laughed, gently slapping his arm. "You can have the couch. I just think we have to find this man. We have to fix this, and we're not going to do it at four in the morning. We can run home, sleep a few hours, and then figure out our next steps."

He couldn't help but match her enthusiasm, "Okay, girl, whatever you say."

That night, April's dreams came to life. She watched with an unknown audience as a bearded man, weighted down in chains like the spirit of *A Christmas Carol's* Jacob Marley, moved slowly across the stage toward a glass coffin, with David inside. She watched as the bearded man threw himself against the coffin, chains clanking against cracking glass, until finally, the coffin shattered, releasing David, who pounced on the man with the strength of a lion, relenting only when the man's pleas filled the silent auditorium.

"Release me," he wailed, sinking to his knees. "Free me from this hell. Break these chains or break me, but I can't go on like this."

David paced the stage, an internal battle gnawing at his soul. He stopped, standing over the broken glass, then dropped to his knees and began picking up the pieces, painstakingly putting them together. With bleeding hands, he rebuilt the coffin, climbed inside, and pulled the top closed.

The curtain fell as April's eyes fluttered open.

DAY 6

She lay in her bed for another hour, considering this new dream and its meaning when her mother's voice drew her downstairs.

"April," the shout came from the living room. She ran down the stairs, taking two at a time, where she found Maye in her robe holding a fire poker and David standing with his hands up in surrender.

"Mom!" she yelled, grabbing the weapon, "what are you doing? That's David."

"Well, forgive me for protecting my home against intruders." Maye responded tightening her robe. "Even if he is a handsome one. A little warning would be nice next time. I don't always wear a robe, or pajamas."

April shook her head, trying to free herself from the image forming in her mind. "David, meet my thankfully clothed mother Maye, who apparently thinks she's a Viking. Mom, this is David, the new friend I told you about."

"Pleasure." Maye snuffed. "Who needs coffee?" Without waiting for an answer, she left the room."

"I am so sorry, she can be crazy."

"I heard that," echoed from the kitchen.

David laughed, folding the blankets on the couch. "I don't blame her. I would have reacted the same way. At least, she thinks I'm handsome." He winked.

"Don't feel too good about that. She's easy to impress."

"Ouch."

April picked up the remaining unfolded blanket. Trying to decide if she should share her dream. Deciding against it, she asked, "Do you like omelets? I can make some, or french toast, or there's cereal if you'd prefer."

"Omelets sound great. I'm not much for cooking, but I can chop vegetables."

While they prepared breakfast, Maye sat at the table, interrogating David as he chopped.

"Where are you from?"

"Kansas."

"Why are you here?"

"Still trying to figure that out, but I think April is part of it."

"Yes, she told me about your thing. How long has that been happening?"

"Years."

"Does it always work?"

"I believe so."

"What are your intentions with my daughter? Are you the take it and break it type?"

"Mom," April interjected, while David grinned amused.

"Well, it's a fair question. A week ago, he shows up in the street randomly, then yesterday not a word, and now he's sleeping over and making breakfast.

"She's got a point." David said, popping a piece of bell pepper in his mouth.

"Don't encourage her." April whispered toward him under her breath.

"At least, he's got the good sense to know how crazy this all is."

April watched as her mother poured another cup of coffee, whisking eggs in a bowl.

"You're right. I should apologize to both of you. April, I am truly sorry for worrying you yesterday, and, Maye, please forgive me for the unexpected intrusion."

"You're forgiven, but you still haven't answered my question."

April felt a flush creep to her face as David caught her eyes. "Well, ma'am, I'm not sure exactly what the future holds. But I'll tell you, now that I've met her, I don't think I'd ever be happy without her in my life."

"Was that so hard, April?"

"Enough, Mom, how about we make it through today before we plan anything else."

"Ouch," David said again with a grin.

That sound ominous. "What's today?"

April looked at David, unsure of how to answer.

"April and I have a man to find."

"Oh, exciting. Do you have to take something from this mystery man?"

This time, David looked to April. "Mom, it's a long story. How about we save it for another time?"

"Well, it's only eight in the morning. You two have all day. Let's eat and find something to do. We can even get lunch downtown. Then you two can have your little adventure without me in your way."

Laughing, April flipped the eggs in the skillet. "We haven't even had breakfast yet, what are we going to do until lunch?"

"Church!" David exclaimed.

"Church?" April and her mother responded in unison.

"Yes, church. I haven't been in a church in years, and I could use the peace that comes from being in God's house."

"Years? I thought you were all Bible thumper."

"Mom!"

"Again, she's got a point, April."

"Don't encourage her." April giggled.

"That's another long story, Maye. Hopefully, there will be a time in our futures to explain. There's got to be a church nearby."

"Oh, there is. First something or other, Baptist? Presbyterian? Who can remember these things?" Maye said, taking a long slurp from her mug.

"That'll do!"

She stood in awe of the church. It was beautiful inside and out. At the door, they were greeted by two ladies about her age and directed to the coffee station. Her mother and David were eager to accept more coffee, but she was worried it might make her need to pee, and she didn't want to get up during the service.

The sanctuary was huge. Rows of padded seats making a semi-circle around the stage, and fall decorations (harvest not Halloween) were tastefully placed. She followed David who moved confidently to the third row and motioned for April and Maye to enter before him. They began to sit when a tall thin man in skinny jeans and shiny shoes led the band on stage. He motioned the audience to rise, welcomed the guests, and began strumming his guitar.

April looked around the room, feeling a bit awkward to be the only one in this sea of people who didn't seem to know the words to the songs. They were displayed on a screen, but she couldn't keep up, and decided to just listen instead of trying to sing along.

During the second song, she noticed people putting their arms in the air. Wondering what it meant, she turned to David, who had his eyes closed, one hand in the air, and his lips moving fervently, not in pace with the current song. *Must be a Psalm*, she thought. She looked next to her mother, who looked stiff and uncomfortable, then turned back to the front, closing her eyes and listening to the words of the song. She felt a small stirring in her heart and opened her eyes, distracted by a thought she couldn't place.

The guitar player stepped up to the mic, as a melody formed behind him saying, "Some of you here today are trapped in bondage. It might be a situation, or distraction, or a lie that you are not enough, but let me tell you the good news. We serve a God, a father, who is bigger than your situation, your fears, and any lie that might be holding you down. A God who loves you and seeks you, and there is nothing he won't do to get to you." The title of the next song, "Reckless Love," flashed on the screen, followed by words that boasted of a God who was not only willing but also eager to overcome any obstacle on his way to your heart.

She felt her mind begin to spin as her heart quickened at the thought of a God who loved her so much he would chase her in ways that didn't seem to make sense. Ways like sending a man to a bar to take her addiction and free her from herself. She thought of the past six years since she had first left home and the number of times she should have been dead, and how somehow despite all of that, she was here alive next to a man who was sent by a God she desperately wanted to know. She wasn't sure if it was allowed in church, but she couldn't help reaching over and clutching David's hand. He squeezed hers tightly as if in agreement.

When the worship and announcements ended, the pastor took the stage. He opened the sermon by directing parishioners to Ezekiel 24, telling the room that today's message would be about the contrast between obedience and disobedience and how emotions can impact the outcome. He explained the backstory of this chapter, describing the ruins God planned to make of Jerusalem due to the people's actions. He described the impurity of the people and their unwillingness to turn from their ways and follow the law, and how God spoke through Ezekiel the prophet, telling them that his judgment would fall according to their actions.

"Now let's move into verse fourteen. In this verse, Ezekiel tells of a word he received from God, you'd think it's got to get better, right? Not for our friend, Ezekiel. In this vision, God tells Ezekiel that his wife is going to die. The Bible uses the term 'delight of your eye.'" David squeezed her hand again as the pastor continued. "We don't know if it's speaking to her looks or her place of affection in Ezekiel's life, but either way, we know that he loves her dearly. Here's where it gets 'weird.' God tells Ezekiel not to weep or cry, or follow any of the traditional mourning practices in this time. They typically made a big display of loss, if you don't believe me check out Job." Laughter filled the room. "Keep in mind here, God isn't saying not to be sad. He's saying keep the emotion in check, continue on in the work that you've been called to. Obey. Ezekiel did just that. When his wife died the following day and Ezekiel stayed true to God's command, the people were freaked out. They didn't understand his reaction or what this had to do with them. The original millennials. Can I get an amen?" More laughter mixed with amen. "So, our boy Ezekiel explained to them that God would destroy Jerusalem, the delight of their eyes. You see, the people didn't believe God would destroy Jerusalem since it was the home of his temple, his chosen place, and their emotional connection to the city blinded them to God's truth. Now to top it all off, Ezekiel is telling them that they must respond in the same way, with obedience. Let's look at verses twenty-five to twenty-seven, 'And you, son of man, on the day I take away their stronghold, their joy and glory, the delight of their eyes, their heart's desire, and their sons and daughters as well on that day a fugitive will come to tell you the news. At that time your mouth will be opened; you will speak with him and will no longer be silent.' So, you will be a sign to them, and they will know that I am Lord."

April sat up straighter in her seat. For some reason, those words struck a chord in her soul. David looked at her curiously as she pulled out her phone to bookmark those verses in her app.

"My point here, folks, is that your feelings don't change God's will. The people had a chance, and they made a choice to disobey, and that choice led to the destruction of Jerusalem. So I tell you, it's your time to make a choice. You can choose to obey God's will in your life, or not. As we invite the worship team back to the stage, please stand and bow your heads. I am welcoming you now to make a decision to join the family and accept Christ into your life as your Lord and savior. For some of you, it may be for the first time and for others, it may be renewing your commitment. If either one applies, I'd like you to take a step of faith and put your hand in the air. Be bold. I see you over there, thank you. Yes, I see you too."

April felt a calling in her heart, like a whisper from her father asking her to come home. Her chest clenched at the thought of raising her hand. What would the people around her think?

"Again, I say, be bold. Lift your hand if you need Jesus in your heart. Your father is calling you today. Chose now to obey. Don't let fear hold you down. Lift your hand and speak these words with me."

April's heart stirred again, a rush of emotions flying through her spirit—doubt, fear, and desire. Her desire to know God overcame her fear, and she slipped her hand up, feeling an intense calm as she spoke the words, accepting Christ as her savior. When the prayer ended, the band began to play again. This time, she sang along.

When they returned to the house, after filling up at the Olive Garden, Maye excused herself for a nap, while April and David planned how to find the mystery man. David poured them both coffees as April opened a laptop on the table. He couldn't help but smile as the sun shone its afternoon light on her face. He thought about how much she had changed from the night he had first met her. The dark makeup and big hair were replaced by her natural beauty and a simple braid. She had given up whatever façade she had been putting on, allowing her hope-filled innocence to rise to the surface. If he had thought her lovely that night, his opinion had since grown a hundred-fold in the recent days, her inner beauty shining so brightly he almost had to look away.

"What?" she asked, looking at him.

"Uh. Sorry. I got distracted. Coffee coming right up." He placed the mugs on the table as she looked at him with skepticism.

"How do we even start, David? This is like finding a specific hair on a walrus."

He chuckled at the unusual simile. "Well, we know he's local and probably, the general area he lives in. Not many people go out of their way to find a park bench hidden in an apartment complex."

"You did."

"Touché, but I am the anomaly not the norm. Besides, I didn't exactly go looking for a park, I kind of just landed there."

"Okay, then where is the park?"

"Another good question. It's within a three hour or so walk from the hotel."

She slammed the laptop lid down, making him jump and spill his coffee. "Sorry," she said, sheepishly handing him a napkin. "I just don't know where to start. Spokane has over two hundred thousand people. How do we even begin? Is your compass thing working yet?"

"Nope. Nothing, not even a blip."

"Well, then maybe we change our approach. Maybe we try to figure out who he is instead of finding where he is. What do you remember about him?"

He thought back to that night, trying to picture the man. "It was dark, April. I don't remember much. He seemed short and was stocky. Not like chubby, just a square man. He had a beard, and I think his hair was dark, lighter than yours but not blonde. He must have been in his midthirties, and I remember thinking about his eyes. They were haunted and almost sunken back into his head."

"Was he slightly balding, with a broad chest, and weird purple bags under his eyes?" she asked.

"Yes, I think so. How would you even know that?"

"Oh my god, um, gosh. David, it's Stephen."

"Stephen?"

"Yes." She stood and began pacing. He had accepted this as her thinking posture. "When you texted me last night, I was at Phil's. I didn't tell you because I didn't want you to think I was drinking, I wasn't. I just needed to get out of here. I couldn't sleep, and I just had coffee. So, I went down there. I guess I was hoping maybe you'd be there, but then you weren't there—"

"April," he interjected. "Stephen?"

"Yeah, so I'm at Phil's and after eleven thirty or so, the place is mostly empty, but there's this guy sitting at the end of the bar, says he's new in the area. I'm telling you, he sounds just like you described. The haunted look is what made me think of him. He had these thick purple bags under his eyes, like he hadn't slept in years.

David felt the fingers of a memory poking at his mind again. "April, I think I saw him that night, before the park, sitting in the same stool back by the swinging doors. I thought the compass was pointing to Bee, but it was him all along. I can't believe I didn't recognize him. What else did he say?"

April stopped moving, resting her hands on the back of the chair. "Not much. He's Stephen, from Missouri and has only been here a few months. He made some comment about a woman at the bar leaving with some random guy, but it was generic, like 'that was easy.'"

David felt a pit rise from his stomach to his throat, finally grasping the memory that had been eluding him for so many days; his hands forming fists on the table. He slammed them down. This time, causing April to jump, as ice formed in his blood.

"What, David, what?" She stared at him, unblinking, waiting for his response. But he couldn't answer. He thought back to the nauseated feeling he had felt at the bar when seeing the man. The way he had been unmoved by the man's sobs in the park and back to the first time he had seen the man's face. Skinnier back then, without the beard, and on a mugshot in his sister's file.

He couldn't hold back the flood that poured from his eyes, the second time he had cried for her since her death. Standing, he started for the door. Unable to stop himself, he bellowed, "He killed my sister."

He felt the door slam behind him.

She stood, shocked by his sudden revelation, unsure of whether or not to follow.

"Go," Maye said from the hallway. "Don't let him leave. He might not come back." Maye entered the kitchen, pulling April into a quick hug.

"I don't know what to say, Mom."

"It doesn't matter what you say. He loves you. Now it only matters what you do. Go, follow him." Her mother pushed her toward the door, and April didn't stop. She ran out of the house, taking the steps in one bound and caught up to David at the corner of the street.

"Stop, please stop," she said, grabbing his arm. When he turned to her, his eyes were red and swollen. A vein stood out on his forehead, and his hands were clenched. "Stop," she whispered. She stared at him, trying to find words to say, when he collapsed into her. She stumbled back, unprepared for his weight, gripping him as he sobbed. "Tell me."

"I can't." He forced the words through his sobs.

"David, you have to. There's something happening here and you have to face it, but you don't have to face it alone." She led him slowly back to the house, guiding him to the table where Maye had poured three glasses of whiskey.

"Mom," she scolded, putting David in a chair.

"Stop," Maye answered sternly. "One drink will calm the nerves and settle us all. We don't need to get drunk. Moderation and what not."

David gulped back the amber liquid and slammed the glass on the table with such ferocity she thought it might break in his hands. She thought briefly back to her dream, his hands covered in blood as he pieced together the glass coffin. Pushing the thoughts away, she said, "How? How did he kill your sister?"

He sat in silence. Maye sipping her drink, April nervously turning her glass on the table, until he finally relented.

"Hope was such a happy girl," he started, then pushed his glass toward Maye for a refill. "We were twins. She was the happy bright one, while I was moodier and introvert. I always felt off, being what I am, but she knew the gifts God gave me and never accused me of depression like my parents did. In fact, when all of my parent's attempts at making me 'normal' failed, Hope was able to make me laugh. She went out and bought a ukulele, learned to play, and would come in and sing silly songs to me. Eventually, she saved up to buy a guitar for me, and we started writing and singing songs together. Her voice was as beautiful as her soul. At that time in my life, it was the only true joy that I felt. When my parents sent me to summer camp, where I met Caleb, it was Hope's idea, and it probably saved my life."

He paused, taking another drink. "After camp, she convinced me to join the worship team so we could play together, and we did for the next five years. I was able to overcome other people's emotions by focusing on her light. She was the beacon guiding me to God, while Caleb was the one helping me to understand what it all meant. And the way she prayed, it was fierce. She was a warrior and believed in God's power like nobody I've met since, so I should have known something was wrong when her light started to fade. No, it didn't fade. It just went out completely. She stopped showing up to church and family dinners, broke up with her boyfriend of three years without reason, and just stopped talking to everyone. I was an idiot and thought something had happened between her and Bryon. I should have known. I should have felt something was wrong."

Finishing his second glass, he let his face fall in his hands. April pushed her untouched drink toward him, silently begging for him to continue. He did. "After three months, I finally broke down the door to her apartment, literally. She was a mess—disheveled and dirty, unable to speak coherently. There were empty liquor bottles everywhere (he held up his glass ironically). Still, somehow, I thought it was all related to the breakup. We fought. She threw a bottle at me, and I wrote her off. I told her to stop being so dramatic, to toughen up and move on. And then I left. Two days later, she was found by a friend. Dead. She had taken a handful of sleeping pills, washed down with tequila, the very night I was there. I could have stopped it, should have. Like that, she was gone.

The air in the room was heavy. April felt claustrophobic, unable to move or speak. Maye poured herself another glass and lifted the bottle toward April, who shook her head no. Instead, she reached across the table and clutched David's hand. He squeezed hers tightly before continuing.

"A few weeks later, a detective showed up at my parent's while I was there. It was after her funeral. Sanchez. He didn't know that I didn't know, so he told my parents that a man had been caught in connection to Hope's case. His name was Stephen Foster. His DNA matched with assaults on two other girls. He'd raped her, taken her virginity, humiliated her, and filled her with an overwhelming shame. She didn't tell any of us. My parents only knew because she'd listed my mom as her emergency contact. She was trapped in her own hell, feeling dirty and ashamed, and couldn't tell us. She couldn't tell me. I should have known, should have been there. Instead, after I left her house, I followed the arrow. I was taken to Kansas City, to a bar with Allen, a hedge fund manager who was facing jail time for fraud. The night my sister took her life, I prevented Allen from taking his. I swore to God that I would always fulfill his purpose, would always love him, but I haven't prayed since that night. How do you tell God that you're angry with him? How do you believe that he has a plan but in the face of that tell him you don't understand why he let something like that happen to somebody so good and so pure? Why did Allen deserve to find peace, when my sister found death?"

He tilted his head up, finishing the last of her whiskey. A look of desperation set on his face in stone.

April left her seat, dropping in front of his on her knees, wrapping her arms around him, and said, "I would take this from you. I would take it all, your hurt and pain and memories. I would take it if I could."

His body fell over hers as he wept.

When his tears finally subsided, Maye helped her move him to the couch, where he fell into a restless sleep. She sat on the ground beside him, her hand holding tightly to his, and prayed to God for freedom for this man she loved so dearly.

When he left the couch several hours later, he was consumed by a hurricane of emotions, sadness for the memory of his sister's death, conflict for his assigned task, and desire for the potential of a future, not just wandering but an actual life; something he hadn't imagined possible in years.

When he entered the kitchen, he found April at the computer and Maye standing behind with a pen and notebook. They had taken on his cause. Part of him was overwhelmed at their love toward him, but another part fought to push them away. This wasn't their battle and who knew what consequence might fall on them because he unintentionally brought them into it.

April looked up as he entered, asking, "You feeling okay?"

"Torn," he answered honestly.

She turned the laptop toward him, an image of the bearded man covering the monitor. "We were trying to learn more about him," she said, almost sheepishly. "He plead guilty to two counts of rape, taking a plea for five and a half years. After he was released from Leavenworth, there's not much on him."

"We do know he was married at the time of his conviction," Maye added.

"What kind of monster is he?" David asked, taking a chair.

"This is where it gets interesting." April pulled up another webpage. "Like I said, after he was released from prison, there's nothing on him. He pretty much disappears off the face of earth. But while he was in prison, a local news station did a sort of 'in the mind of a criminal' documentary on him, and I'll be honest. It's bleak. The guy had a hell of a childhood, literally."

She turned the computer toward him, giving a summary as he read, "He grew up in a totally abusive house. His parents were both raging alcoholics who beat him relentlessly during their binges for fun. When he was twelve, the state finally investigated at the insistence of a teacher, and he was removed from their care and placed with an aunt. From the looks of it, things were okay until that aunt remarried, and well, I'll let you read the rest." She got up to pace as he continued reading.

The article detailed how the boy's life worsened. His uncle was later arrested for sexual assault, after three years of sexually torturing the boy. At sixteen, he was put into a series of foster homes, never lasting long as he was declared violent and dangerous. Eventually, he landed in juvenile detention after being charged with aggravated assault, where he stayed attending court-ordered therapy and taking mood-stabilizing prescriptions. When he was finally released, he managed to have a somewhat normal life, even getting married and having a child, while maintaining a job in pest control, until his uncle passed away. According to the article, the uncle's death had caused Stephen to quit his medications and his job, and sent him into a spiral, which resulted in his spree of criminal activity.

David rubbed his hands on his temple, trying to process what he had read, then looked to April helplessly. "It's a sad story."

She sat at the table again. "I have to tell you something."

He looked back at her, expectantly.

"I've been having dreams about you."

Maye nodded.

"And?" he asked, not sure what to expect.

April told him about how the dreams started, just the two of them meeting, like replaying a memory. "But then they changed. I started seeing you trapped in a glass box. You looked terrified." She paused again, looking to Maye, who nodded again. "Then last night, it changed. I saw this man who I know now was Stephen, and he was covered in chains. He was so broken and so desperate, David. He started banging the chains against your glass coffin until it shattered. He was begging you to help him, to release him, but you refused. You turned away from him and rebuilt the coffin with the pieces of broken glass. Your hands were covered in blood, and then once it was back together, you climbed back in it."

"And then?" he asked.

"That's it. It ended."

"April, what are you saying?"

She began pacing again. "It's not what *I'm* saying. I think it's what God's saying."

"Which is what?"

She stopped. Meeting his eyes, she answered, "You have to help him."

"Come on, April. After what he did to Hope? You want me to just forget all about that?"

"Yes. Isn't that exactly what Jesus was all about? I know I don't know much, but I know forgiveness was kind of his thing."

"April," he started, but she interrupted, the fire in her eyes closing his mouth.

"David, if you don't, you'll never be free. You'll live the rest of your life choosing to stay trapped in that box with blood on your hands."

He stared back at her. The fury rising again in his throat, unable to respond.

Maye took the chair next to him pulling it closer to him and grasped his hands with sadness in her eyes. "I don't know your God, hon, or your past, but I do know you are at a crossroads and like the pastor said this morning, you have to make a choice. Your feelings about this don't change God's will. It won't be easy, but April is right."

He looked from Maye to April, who stood with her arms crossed, then suddenly, she shouted, "The verses." And ran out of the room. When she returned, she was carrying an old beat-up Bible. She plopped it down on the table and began thumbing through the pages, muttering "Ezekiel" under her breath. "Ah ha!" she said when she had finally found the verses she had been searching for. "Look." She pointed to verse twenty six. "The fugitive. God said the fugitive would come and tell about the destruction, and on that day, his mouth would be opened. Don't you see, David? This is your fugitive. This is your chance to be free."

He read the words again. Reading of Ezekiel's loss and his obedience in the face of that loss. "I'll try."

It was nearly seven when they had finally made a plan to find the bearded man. April could see the exhaustion in David's face and worried he might change his mind. They still had two hours before they would head back to Phil's to see if they could find Stephen. If he wasn't at Phil's, they would try to find their way back to the park. If David's compass wasn't working, then April would pray, and they would search until they found him. April couldn't shake the feeling that they were running out of time.

Maye decided to make dinner. She couldn't handle sitting around. While Maye stayed busy, April and David sat at the table, David sharing his favorite psalms.

"Why do you like these so much?" April asked.

"Most of them were written by King David, who I was named after. David was considered a man after God's own heart, and I guess I've always wanted to live up to that. He spent a lot of time on the run. In fact, many of these verses were written while he was hiding in caves, while his father-in-law was trying to kill him."

"Maybe," she said, "we should read some of these. I'll keep praying, but I think it will help you find comfort. This isn't going to be an easy night."

"No." He agreed. "I don't think it will. Let's start in Psalm one hundred eighteen." He read out loud the verses that he had taken comfort in so many times before.

"Give thanks to the Lord, for he is good; his love endures forever. Let Israel say: "His love endures forever." Let the house of Aaron say: "His love endures forever." Let those who fear the Lord say: "His love endures forever." When hard pressed, I cried to the lord; he brought me into a spacious place. The Lord is with me; I will not be afraid. What can mere mortals do to me? The lord is with me; he is my helper. I look in triumph on my enemies."

"Amen," April said, when he had finished the chapter.

"Amen," Maye echoed from the oven.

She could tell he was still worried. Deep crevasses in his brow gave that away. So, she whispered another prayer, just for him.

They sat in silence while they ate.

By the time dinner was eaten and the dishes were nearly cleaned, he had a thin layer of sweat covering his forehead. He knew April was concerned for him. She wouldn't say it, but he could feel the weight of her eyes watching him. For years after Hope's death, he had thought about the vile villain of a man who had caused her so much pain. Always seeing in his mind the image from the police files. Along the way, his brain had twisted that face to resemble a monster more than a man, and now he would have to face that monster—his very own Goliath. Now, instead of reacting with the revenge his heart yearned for, he was being asked to take from that man some pain or burden. A battle raged in his mind. Right versus wrong, love over hate. He felt the sweat dripping down his temple and wiped it away with the back of his hand.

"David?" she asked, drying a plate. It was as though she could see the battle on his face.

"Hmm?"

"What can I do?"

"Help me find him."

"Are you sure?"

"Yes."

"What will you do?"

He sighed, hands dripping with soapy water pressed against the sink. "I don't know," he answered at last.

"What can I do?"

"Help me find him."

She nodded, holding steadfast his gaze. "I'll stay with you."

Returning his attention to the plates, "I don't know if you can."

"Wait. What? What do you mean?"

"April, the first time I saw him in the bar and then again in the park, I was filled with an unimaginable rage, like I've never experienced before. Even as he wept, I felt no pity for him, and that was before I knew who he was. I'd like to think that I will show grace when I meet him face to face, but part of me is worried I'll come unhinged. Your dream may have been quite literal when it ended with blood on my hands." He felt it again, the heavy weight of her gaze on him.

"You couldn't, though."

"I could."

"But you wouldn't."

He sighed again. "I don't know. I dreamt of destroying him, April. Hope was a light, a beacon. So full of joy and grace, and he snuffed that out. He didn't take her life, but he might as well have. In my book, he's guilty of murder."

He felt now the weight of her hand on his arm. "David. I've been reading about your King David and I think," she paused, searching his face. "Well, actually, I know that he did some bad things. He even had a man killed."

"April," he began.

"No—" she interrupted. "You can't pick and choose which parts about him you like."

He pulled away from her, frustration rising to his chest. "What's your point?"

"My point is, you have the whole picture now, but I bet there were times when people thought *he* was a monster. You are only seeing one moment of Stephen's life. It's clear to me that God has a purpose for this man. Why else would he send you? What he did was terrible, but God's grace is bigger than that. I…um." She stepped toward him again, lifting her hand toward his face, then letting it drop as she fumbled, "Saving him will save you."

She wanted so badly to touch him, but she didn't. She kept her hands at her sides waiting for his response.

"I don't know if it's worth it," he finally answered.

"It has to be. It's not just you now. It's me too, and I know every time I see you, I'll know that you could have helped and didn't. It's been less than a week, six days, David, but that's all the time I need to know the type of man you are. The type of man I am unexplainably in love with, and I know that to be this man, you have to do what's right. You can't have it both ways."

His head dropped, as if considering the weight of those words. Shaking it, he looked up at her again. "I don't know if I can be who you think I am."

"I don't think you are, David. I know you are. Who have you been all this time? You go around following God obediently, living every day to take on the next task. What type of man does that, if not a good one?"

"A lost one."

"You are not lost. You are the most found person I've ever met in my life, irritatingly so."

"April, all of these things I do, I do it knowing that God is good and trusting in his goodness, but I also do it to avoid living a life as the man who failed to save his sister, don't you get that?"

"You didn't fail to save her. It wasn't your job to save her. Don't *you* get that?"

His eyebrows raised in a surprised arch.

"David, I'm sorry. I didn't mean that. I mean I did. But not like that."

"No. You're right," he responded. "We're running out of time. Let's get ready."

In her room, she dressed in comfortable fall clothes—jeans, tennis shoes, a long sleeve shirt, with a light hoodie, and a jacket just in case. She thought about what she had said, never one able to hold her tongue, and shook her head in embarrassment. He had to know though, right? That it wasn't his fault. That in life, bad things just happened sometimes, and the blame is on the person doing the bad thing. She felt like she was betraying him. How could she ask him to face this man, this monster that he had fled from?

"April," he called from the stairs. "Come on."

She wanted to run to him. To apologize. To tell him that everything would be okay, but she couldn't. So, she walked slowly and deliberately out of the room, keeping her head down and hands at her side.

"April," he said again as she walked past. "April, stop." He slipped his fingers into hers. "I'm sorry," he said.

"I'm sorry too. I sometimes open my mouth when I should keep it shut."

"No, you were right."

"Does that mean you're going to do it?"

"I don't know what's going to happen."

As they drove, he couldn't stop looking at her. He was amazed by her calm confidence. He thought back to the first night he had met her—on an empty street, surrounded by thick walls and a heavily guarded heart. He had never imagined that night how that scared little girl would have changed so drastically into the strong woman who was now driving him to his future. For better or worse, this night would change the course of his life.

The trip was a short one. Like usual, the street was all but empty, so they parked directly in front of Phil's. As she stopped the engine and reached for the door handle, he grabbed her hand saying, "Wait."

She sat back in her seat, looking at him expectantly. He wanted to tell her he loved her, to scream it from the rooftops. He wanted to beg her to drive away, to forget this mission and run away with him to the mountains, but he couldn't. Instead, he said, "I need to go in alone." Her face fell, and it killed him. He would never want to disappoint her, but if this was it and if things didn't go how she wanted them to, he couldn't let her see the man he feared he might become.

"I'm sorry," he said, pushing the door open.

The music from the jukebox hit him when the door swung open. A popular melody that usually appealed to him now felt hollow when it landed on his ears. He glanced around the near empty bar, his eyes finally landing on a dark form sitting in the shadows at the furthest corner of the bar. A dark hoodie pulled up over his head, hid his features.

David stared at the dark form, at the man who had destroyed his sister and his family. He imagined not the forlorn face of the young man from the mug shot but instead pictured a grisly monster. A green faced demon hiding in the dark. He was unable to move. Fear clutching his heart, making him a statue glued to the door. He wasn't afraid of the man. He was afraid of the decision he was about to make.

He was tempted to leave, to go back to the car and get April, but he knew he had to do this alone. He took a step and then another, never feeling more alone than he did now, surrounded by the empty laughter of complete strangers. As he neared the man, something felt off. He couldn't place it. Nervous to sit too close, he left a seat between them. The man glanced toward him saying with a look of surprise, "You're April's new dude."

April sat in the car, nervously tapping her fingers on the wheel as minutes passed by on the neon clock. She felt like it was mocking her. Deliberately refusing to show the next minute. First five and then ten minutes passed, each one dragging on. Nothing.

How long will this take? she thought, pushing away the urge to burst into Phil's metaphorical guns blazing. But he was right. He would have to do this alone. She would only be a distraction. So, her fingers continued to drum the wheel. Finally, what seemed like an eternity later, light broke through the door frame, David's form blocking her view into the bar. He walked toward the car while the light faded, until only his outline was visible in the dark night. She couldn't contain her energy and blurted out, "So?" before the door was completely open.

He slid into the empty passenger seat, closing the door behind him before answering, "Kyle says hi."

"What?"

"Kyle told me to tell you hello, and he misses seeing you around. Also said something about your ex looking for you but assured me I was better than that low-life thug."

She watched as a loose grin lit up his tense face and couldn't help but laugh. They say laughter is infections, which proved to be true as David's laughter soon joined her own. They laughed until tears streamed down both of their face.

"Are…," she stammered. "Are you serious?"

"I am." He assured her, wiping the tears from his face with his jacket sleeve.

"What happened?"

"I thought it was Stephen, and I was so scared of exploding, but then it was this skinny, wannabe gangster-looking kid. His hood was up, and he was wearing one of those puffy jackets that made him look stockier. I think he thought I was a cop coming to bust him. The worst part is, he gave it all up. Totally ratted himself out thinking you'd already turned him over to the Feds."

Laughter filled the car again. This time followed by an uneasy silence.

"What now?" April asked.

He threw up his hands. "I don't know. I guess we stick to the plan and try to find the park. She nodded in agreement and turned the key.

It took about fifteen minutes to locate the right apartment complex. David had a general idea of the direction and was able to navigate with relative ease. After a few wrong turns, he finally pointed out the entrance to Pine Village. They parked in a spot labeled "Visitors" and began to walk toward the center of the complex.

"It's kind of spooky," she said, zipping her sweater against the cool September wind. "It seems so deserted."

He took her hand as they walked, responding, "I felt the same way the last time I was here.

The park was empty when they approached, and she could feel the weight of disappointment settle on David's shoulders. "It's not over yet," she said, squeezing his hand. They decided to sit in the shadows on an old creaky swing set to avoid deterring Stephen should he come.

They swung in silence for a moment before David finally spoke. "April, I want to ask you something, but I don't want to freak you out."

She looked toward him, but his focus remained on the empty bench. "I want you to come back with me to Kansas. I was serious when I told your mom I couldn't imagine my life without you. This week, despite the sadness and pain, has been filled with more joy than I've felt since Hope's death. You've reminded me that there is so much more than going from place to place, and while I've been doing what God called me to, I've been doing it out of obligation. I think that God brought me to you, or maybe sent you to me to remind me of the power of love. I wouldn't have the strength to do what I have to do with you beside me."

Her words caught in her throat as the truth of his revelation hit her. She wanted to agree, to tell him she would follow him anywhere, but instead, she dropped her head. Thinking of who she had been before the night she had met him, she felt dirty and unworthy, pictures of her past flashing through her mind like a picture show.

"April?"

"David, you don't know me. You don't understand the things I've done, the person I've been." She shuddered, not from the cold but in remembrance of her life before.

He grabbed the chain on her swing, twisting her toward him. "Don't you get it, April? I don't care where you came from. I can see your future. You will be a mighty warrior of God, a light in these dark places, the light I need."

She jumped out of the swing, moving away from him. "It's easy to say that now." She cried. "You don't know. But what happens when you get curious? What happens when you find out I've traded sex for drugs, practically a whore! It's easy when you're facing a challenge, to believe that these things don't matter but when this is behind you, when life is mundane and we're out of this weird bubble, what then?

"Mary Magdalene," he said quietly.

"What?" she stopped and stared at him.

"Mary Magdalene had seven demons in her before she met Christ."

"What's your point?"

"After she met Christ, she became his avid follower. Jesus didn't care what she had been before, he cared about who she was. You are not the sum of your mistakes. We all battle demons, you in your way and me in my own. It doesn't make you less worthy of love. In fact, maybe you need someone like me who has years of pent up love to give."

She turned her back to him to hide her tears. "But you don't know," she whispered, choking back sobs. She heard the soft crunch of gravel under his feet and felt his warmth as he wrapped his arms around her.

"I forgive you," he said. "And I promise I will never hold your past against you."

She turned toward him, his eyes glistening as he continued. "Six days ago, I asked you to let me take something from you and you did. And in this week, our lives have been so much better, just because of this unity we've shared. So, now I'm asking you to let me give you something. Will you let me love you for everything you are, everything you've been, and everything you will become?"

She nodded, resting her head on his chest. She listened to the beat of his heart and found herself filled with peace. "Thank you, God," she whispered. Pulling away from him, she wiped the tears from her eyes. "David?" she asked. "Will you forgive him? Stephen, I mean. Even if we don't find him, will you forgive him?" She saw his jaw clench and his muscles stiffen. Placing her hand over his heart, she continued, "Don't do it for him, do it for you. I'm starting to think this whole thing isn't about him. He was God's way of changing you. Will you let it go? Release yourself from the hold he's had on you for nearly seven years. In the name of Jesus, let it go."

As he listened to her pleas, a battle raged in his mind. He was grounded only by her hand over his heart. As she spoke, an unusual warmth flowed through her palm into his chest. He felt his heart beat faster as his vision blurred and a warmth radiated through his body. At some point, he no longer heard her voice. Instead, a booming voice filled his mind, ending the battle. A decision had been reached. The booming voice faded back into April's as she declared, "In the name of Jesus, let it go."

The warmth of her hand was replaced by the familiar pull.

"Let's go," he said, while turning away. He couldn't see it, but he imagined April's face displayed a puzzled look. "Come on," he said over his shoulder. He was already nearly ten feet away from her.

"Wait," she called, finally jogging toward him. "What's happening?"

The pull of the compass was relentless. There was an urgency in it he had never experienced before. "It's back."

"What's back?"

"The compass. Come on, we have to move."

"But, David, the car?"

"Leave it."

The compass pulled them through the complex back to the main road. Persistently tugging through each turn. At one point, he was nearly running and forced himself to slow as April struggled to keep up.

"No way," she said through labored breathing, when the last corner they turned dumped them two blocks down from the neon lights gracing Phil's windows.

In the spot, he had met her six days earlier. He turned to her and said, "I love you, April. No matter what happens next." He kissed her on the forehead, lingering just a moment before the pull of the compass demanded his attention. As they neared the door, he felt again the fear that had clenched his heart just hours earlier. He hesitated, looking to April for guidance. She pushed past him, entering the bar, leaving him no choice but to follow.

When he entered, he nearly ran into her. She had stopped and was staring toward the bar. He followed her gaze until it landed on the man, Stephen. She started to walk toward him, but he grabbed her arm, pulling her back to him. She looked up at him, her eyes searching his face.

"My battle," he said, pointing to a table near the door. "If anything happens, you leave and don't look back."

Defiance shined through her eyes. An eternity passing before her shoulders dropped in surrender, and she took a chair as directed. "I love you." She mouthed as he turned away. She would never know it, but that action gave him the final ounce of courage he needed to approach the bar.

He took a seat near the man, leaving one stool between them as he had earlier.

"What'll you have?" Bones asked from the opposite side of the bar.

"Coffee, black. Thanks."

"Got it."

On his way to the back, Bones stopped in front of Stephen, "Another?"

"Mmm," Stephen muttered.

David fought not to stare. He had expected to see a monster, but here sat a man. A man whose brows were furrowed, eyes sunken, and body weighted down. David could almost see the chains April described from her dream. He had never before felt tentative about approaching a target, but tonight was different.

Stephen turned toward him. "What?" he asked aggressively.

"I'm sorry?"

"You're staring at me."

David paused before answering, "I know you."

The creases in Stephen's forehead deepened. "What? I've never seen you before."

"I was here the other night and I recognized you. I just didn't remember how."

"How?" Confusion had taken over the man's face.

"I remember your picture."

His confusion started to turn to anger. "Look, man, I don't know what this is about, but you need to get the hell away from me."

David folded his hands on the bar, not releasing the man's stare. "I'm David O'Luain." He saw a hint of recognition cross Stephen's face. "Hope was my sister."

"Oh shit." He looked like he was about to flee, eyes darting between David and the door. "Look, man, I did my time. How'd you find me?"

Smiling, David raised his hand out toward the man, who flinched in response to the motion. Any remnants of anger remaining in his soul diminished with Stephen's reflect. Instead of the monster he had seen for so long, he now saw a child who had experienced terrible abuse. A life that had been treated so badly for so long it had adjusted to its circumstance, becoming what it was never meant to be. He dropped his hand.

"Stephen, I forgive you for what you did to Hope. I'm not here for that."

"What are you here for?"

"Let's talk."

April watched, peaking her head over a menu, in her best attempt to hide her observation of the two. She waited while David ordered, worried he might back down. "Lord, give him strength, soften his heart, let him see Stephen in the way that you do." She prayed. She watched as they began to speak, saw a look of terror in the man's eyes, and turned her attention to David, whose eyes softened.

She thought again to the night she met him, overcome with gratitude. She watched as skepticism landed on Stephen's face, remembering her own when David told her about his gift. The menu had fallen to the table, any attempts to hide forgotten, and she clenched her hands in anticipation.

Stephen twirled his drink on the bar in front of him. His muscles tense while he listened to David speak, eyes focused on the dancing glass. She tried to read David's lips but failed. He stood, moved toward Stephen, and placed his hand on the man's trembling shoulder.

She watched as Stephen downed the contents of his glass, picked his jacked from the back of the stool and tugged it on. David stepped back, letting Stephen out of his seat as they started for the exit. Passing her table, David held his palm up toward her, indicating she should stay. Chewing on her lip, she complied.

After they exited, she moved around the table and positioned herself at the window. Peaking over the ledge, she struggled to find them in the shadows. A loud voice drew her gaze to the left, and she pressed her face firmly against the cold window in an attempt to locate the two. The song on the jukebox ended and she heard, "It's too late." Before the next began.

Stephen passed by the window with David on his heel. He turned to face David, giving her a clean line of sight to his face. He had tears in his eyes and a cigarette hanging between his lips. Time dragged as she watched, imagining what David must be saying.

Several minutes passed before Stephen dropped his head. David reached out to him, again placing his hand on the broken man's shoulder. With his head down, she watched as he nodded, accepting the gift that was offered. She watched while David embraced his sister's attacker and witnessed tears of sorrow form streams on the attacker's face.

When David pulled away, the man nodded again, dried his eyes and walked away. David looked toward the window a new strain written on his face. She ran to the exit, bursting through the door, which slammed with a bang behind her.

"David?"

"Not now," he said, walking into the darkness.

Alone now on the street, she called Maye to pick her up. The display on her phone showed 12:01.

DAY 7

Back at the house, Maye brewed a fresh pot of coffee. "Where is he?"

"I don't know, Mom." She threw her spoon on the table in frustration. "I don't know what I expected, but it wasn't this."

"Did he say anything?"

"Nothing important. Just not now."

"Well, you said before that he takes things, right? What exactly does that mean?"

April thought back to what David had told her about the first time he had taken someone's pain, his friend Caleb. "Oh no, Mom!" she said with the realization of what had to happen. "He doesn't just take it, he absorbs it."

"You mean, he...*feels* it?"

"Exactly."

"So right now, he's—"

"Yes."

"April, what can you do?"

"I don't know."

They sat at the table in silence. Each pondering what it would mean to take on the damage of a man like Stephen Foster. She wished now that she had never found the article detailing the man's childhood. Standing, she began to pace.

"April, there's nothing you can do right now. Why don't you try to sleep?"

She wanted to explode at the absurd suggestion. Sleep? Now, while David was out dealing with God knows what? She fought back the urge. "Go to bed, Mom. I'll be all right. I think I'll stay up a bit longer and pray."

"I can stay up with you."

"No, Mom, it's okay. Sleep. I'll wake you if I need you." Maye hesitated, torn between her desire to help her daughter and her need for sleep. April walked to her mother, kneeling down and grasping her mother's hands between her own. "Mom, really. I'm okay. Please go to bed."

Maye allowed April to pull her up from the chair. Once up, her mother gazed lovingly into her eyes for a moment before pulling her into a tight hug. "I'm so happy to have you back." With those words trailing, she left the room.

When April heard the click of her mother's bedroom door, she grabbed the Bible off the table and turned on the small reading lamp that sat next to the couch. Settling in, she whispered, "All right, God. It's just you and me now. Please bring him back to me." She opened the weathered book and searched for the Psalms. Landing on Psalm 34, she began on verse 1. She prayed the words out loud as David had so often done. "I will praise the Lord at all times. I will constantly speak his praises. I will boast only in the Lord; let all who are helpless take heart. Come, let us tell of the Lord's greatness; let us exalt his name together. I prayed to the Lord, and he answered me. He freed me from all my fears. Those who look to him for help will be radiant with joy; no shadow of shame will darken their faces. In my desperation I prayed, and the Lord listened; he saved me from all my troubles. For the angel of the Lord is a guard; he surrounds and defends all who fear him. Taste and see that the Lord is good. Oh, the joys of those who take refuge in him! Fear the Lord, you his godly people, for those who fear him will have all they need. Even strong young lions sometimes go hungry, but those who trust in the Lord will lack no good thing. Come, my children, and listen to me, and I will teach you to fear the Lord. Does anyone want to live a life that is long and prosperous? Then keep your tongue from speaking evil and your lips from telling lies! Turn away from evil and do good. Search for peace, and work to maintain it. The eyes of the Lord watch over those who do right; his ears are open to their cries for help. But the Lord turns his face against those who do evil; he will erase their memory from the earth. The Lord hears his people when they call to him for help. He rescues them from all their troubles. The Lord is close to the brokenhearted; he rescues those whose spirits are crushed. The righteous person faces many troubles, but the Lord comes to the rescue each time. For the Lord protects the bones of the righteous; not one of them is broken! Calamity will surely destroy the wicked, and those who hate the righteous will be punished. But the Lord will redeem those who serve him. No one who takes refuge in him will be condemned."

When she had finished reading the verses, she prayed again for David. Pleas falling through her lips until she surrendered to sleep.

He walked, like he had so many times before. Buildings flashed by him in a blur, the city disappearing behind him until he found himself again at the river. He sat on its soggy bank, ignoring the cold creeping into his bones. As the river tumbled over itself before him, so did his mind.

He was gripped by the weight of another man's actions. Held firmly in the complete recognition of what had been done, not only by the man, but to him, fully immersed in morale bankruptcy. Shame and guilt pressed down on his spirit, accusing him, daring him to step out into the river's angry current. Voices from an unknown past cruelly laughing at 'his' weakness, mocking him relentlessly.

He shook his head, trying to tear free from the rabid claws that gripped at strings in his mind. He was here at this place because it's where Stephen had planned to take his own life on this very night. Even after David had offered, the man didn't believe he was worth it.

"I'm a monster!" he had cried, and now, David understood what he meant. Among the guilt and shame was a desire, no a need for violence. A need to hurt others in a desperate act of self-preservation.

"If you're a monster, others helped to make you that way. You can choose to be more, to be different."

"It's too late," the man cried out. "I can't remember a time before this. My whole life, I was used for entertainment. What more can I be?"

"You can be forgiven."

Now at the water's edge, the rage welled up inside him. As his mind battled against untold acts of violence, he vomited into the bushes. Scrambling to his feet, he slipped, sliding into the mud. Without thought, he began to pound the wet earth beneath him, until mud covered his face, creating an earthen mask and his muscles trembled. He roared out over the river in a desperate attempt to purge the remaining rage.

Still sitting in the mud, shaking in exhaustion and cold, he turned his head to the sky. Tears formed divots in the mud on his face as he shouted toward heaven. "Father, save me from this. Lay your hand upon me and lift this burden from me. Father God, I know you see me, and I know you keep me as one of your own sheep. I'm so lost. Rescue me from this nightmare."

Exhausted, he climbed back up the slope, leaving a trail of mud. He walked until he found a bench, where he collapsed.

She dreamt of him. This time trapped in despair. Walking along a wooded path, until finally finding rest on an old park bench. In her dream, there was an old-style oil lit street lamp that grew brighter and brighter over him while he slept. "Wake up!" She tried to yell to him, but he couldn't hear her. Suddenly, the light became so bright she had to turn her face from the glare. She heard a booming voice command "Go" before the light shattered, shooting her out of her sleep.

The room was still dark. It took her a moment to realize she had fallen asleep on the couch. She rubbed at her temples in the darkness, feeling like she was forgetting something important. Maye must have come down at some point and turned off the light. She had never turned it off, just fallen asleep with the Bible in her hands. She twisted the knob on the lamp, squinting her eyes against the expected onslaught of light. Nothing. Twisting again, she heard a quiet click, but the light had gone out. Sitting in the darkness, she heard a whisper in her mind. "Go." With that word, her dream flooded her mind once again.

"David!" she shouted, scrambling off the couch. She had to get to him. She ran to her purse grabbing her keys before remembering that her car was still parked in a visitor spot at the apartment complex. She glanced at her phone, 4:00 a.m. She had to get to him. Running up the stairs, she slowly entered her mother's room, feeling around in the darkness for the keys to her mother's Volvo.

"April?" Maye murmured. "Is that you?"

"Yeah, Mom, sorry. I think David's in trouble. I have to find him. I need your keys."

"They're in my purse on the back of the door. Give me a minute, and I'll come with you."

"I don't have a minute. I think he's in danger. Turn up the heat and make hot tea. Also, will you put some blankets and towels in the dryer? I'll be back soon."

With that, she ran out of the house.

She drove along river roads for thirty minutes looking for any area that might house a bench. Once she had left the highway, the roads were mostly dark, missing the headlights of early morning commuters and the soft glow of street lamps. She tried to pray while she drove but found herself distracted by large raindrops hitting the windows and the squeal of the wiper blades that wiped them away. Her knuckles gripped the wheel, turning white as she fought back tears that threatened to blind her. *What if I'm too late?* She felt an uneasy sweat begin to form on her brows, quickly rolling down the window as a flood of nausea washed over her.

Paved roads gave way to the soft crunch of wet gravel that demanded she slow her pace, as her tires fought to stick to the wet rocks of the road, threatening to send the vehicle into a fishtail if she turned a corner too quickly. Worry turned into throbbing anxiety, forming in the nape of her neck and rising to her temple. The shadows seemed to mock her, creating shapes in the trees and the black landscape below. She squinted her eyes, trying to decipher the inky legs of shadows from wildlife that lived in the area.

It doesn't make sense, she thought. *This has to be it.* Suddenly, she saw bright orange reflectors signaling a state park entrance. Nearly passing the entrance, she slammed on her breaks and jerked the wheel toward the dirt lane. A large sign warned, "Park Ranger Vehicles Only Beyond This Point." *Screw it*, she thought, navigating her car past the sign.

She drove slowly along the road seeing no benches and no David. Further up, she saw the dim outline of porta potties and a large wooden sign. She pulled up directly in front of the sign, leaving the car running and turning the heat to high. Once out of the car, she pulled her hood over her head and began looking at the sign, which displayed a graphic of the available trails. "Come on!" she mumbled in frustration. "Help me out here." She scanned the map, stopping suddenly as her eyes landed on Old Lantern Trail. "Yes!" The trail was just to the right of the sign. She ran with reckless abandon into the dark path.

The roar of the river became louder the longer she stayed on the trail. The sun, just starting its climb into the sky, provided just enough light to keep her from tripping over loosed branches and rocks. Her shoes and socks were quickly soaked, weighted down by thick mud that clung to the soles. With each twist and turn, she felt her will to run fading. Maybe she was wrong, maybe this was the wrong place. She thought about turning back, her mind overwhelmed by the realization that she was in the forest alone at dawn. "Just a bit further," she told herself, once again trying to pray but unable to through her gasping breaths.

Finally, what seemed like hours to her, but in reality, was a matter of minutes, she saw a clearing up ahead. Her heart fluttered with excitement, as her will was renewed, and her pace quickened again. This had to be it. As she neared, she saw what appeared to be an old wooden bench with a dark figure slumped on it.

"David," she called to him. He was covered in mud, wet, and cold to the touch. She shook him, saying his name over and over again. His eyes slowly rolled open, staring, seeing, but not recognizing. "Come on. You have to get up. I can't carry you. Come on. Let's get warm." Struggling, she pulled him to a sitting position, rubbing his hands between her own. "Come on. You have to get up now."

Slowly, deliberately, she pulled him to his feet. Leading him carefully along the path, back to the car. She was kicking herself for not bringing a blanket. She stripped off her jacket to lay over him. Once in the car, she grabbed his hands again. "You're okay, David. I'm here."

"April," he whispered.

She pulled the car to a screeching stop in the driveway, taking half the time to get back as it had taken to get to the river. By the time she was out of the car, Maye had emerged on the porch.

"Mom, help. Quick." They worked together to get the half-dazed David out of the car.

"What happened?" Maye asked as they carried him to the door.

"I don't know. Will you start the shower? Not too hot, just warm." She gently worked to remove his mud-caked jacket and shirt, covering him in one of the warmed blankets. She stopped awkwardly, unable to bring herself to undress him further; afraid she might cause him embarrassment.

Maye chuckled on the stairs with warm towels in hand. "Odd time to go prude, dear. Come on, help me get him in the bathroom. I'll get him cleaned up."

April blushed. "It's not that, Mom, I just—"

"You don't have to explain. I've been at the nursing home for years. I've given my fair share of sponge baths, admittedly not to anyone this young, or good looking."

"Mom!"

"I'm joking, mostly."

While her mother cleaned David up, she rinsed the mud from his clothes and put them in the washer. She pulled clean sweatpants from his backpack, along with a T-shirt and boxers, handing them through the bathroom door to her mother, then sat at the table with an untouched cup of tea. Exhausted, she laid her head on her arm and closed her eyes.

"April, wake up. Come on, let's get you cleaned up now."

Blinking her eyes against the sun, she allowed her mother to pull her dirty shirt over her head.

"Is he okay?"

"He will be." Maye dipped a washcloth into a bowl of warm soapy water she had set on the table and began to clean the mud off April's face and neck. "He really does love you, you know? Even as a half-asleep popsicle, you're all he'd talk about."

Maye continued to wash April's arms, before sitting on the floor to remove her daughter's shoes and socks. April was too tired to resist. "I love him too, Mama."

"Okay, up to bed now," Maye said after pulling a long nightshirt over April's head and gently braiding her hair. "David's in your bed, so you can lay in mine."

Her eyes closed as her head hit the pillow. Before falling asleep, she smiled hearing her mother say, "Thank you, God, for bringing my girl back to me."

Several hours later, her eyes opened slowly to the sound of a quiet hum. Maye was at her dresser mirror putting on earrings and humming "Amazing Grace." Rolling to her side, April watched her mother with a smile. She couldn't believe that after nearly seven years, she was back in the home she had ran from, without so much as a look back. Watching, she thought back to her childhood, before things had gone so wrong. She thought about the happiness she had felt as a young girl, sitting in this very room with her mother's jewelry box open on the bed, looking through all the beautiful trinkets. She longed for that time, for the closeness they had once shared.

"Good morning, or rather afternoon," Maye said, startling her out of her thoughts. "Did I wake you?"

"No, well yes, but it's okay. I should get up anyways. What time is it?"

"Nearing two."

"Oh my gosh, I haven't slept this late in." She paused, a flush rising to her cheeks. "Well, I guess it hasn't actually been that long, but it feels like ages. A world away from now."

"It certainly does." Maye agreed, sitting on the edge of the bed. "April, if you ever want to tell me about it, you can. You don't have to, but honestly, it was such a shock when you showed up Tuesday morning. Not hearing from you for so long. I guess at some point, I assumed you were just gone. Don't get me wrong, I am thrilled you're back. I just can't believe the little girl that left here has grown into such a wonderful woman.

April blushed. This time, at the compliment. "Honestly, if you'd seen me before last week, you wouldn't be saying that."

Maye moved up the bed and reached for April's arm. "Does it hurt?" she asked, pointing to the scabs and scars.

"Mostly just my pride. They used to bug me all the time, but now they're just a painful reminder of what I was."

"Don't think of them like that. We all have scars, most people's you just can't see. Think of them as a timeline marking who you choose to be now, thanks in part to David."

April sat up straighter in the bed. "David, where is he?"

"He's still asleep, or something like it. I checked on him an hour or so ago. Whatever he's dealing with is putting up a fight. He's been tossing and turning all morning. He's restless, April. I tried to give him water last time I went in, but it's like he's not really there."

"I'm going to go see him." She threw back the covers and climbed out of the bed.

Maye grabbed her arm, stopping her. "Why don't you shower first, and I'll make you some food. There's not much you can do for him right now, and you still have mud in your hair."

April pulled her arm away furiously. "Seriously? You want me to just leave him all alone, while he's like this? This is why Dad left you, you're not capable of love." She watched as her mother's face fell, embarrassed by her outburst. "Mom," she started. Unsure of how to apologize, her words caught in her throat.

"That's not why he left." Maye dropped April's arm. "My problem was never loving him, it was loving myself."

"Oh, Mom, I didn't mean it. I'm just tired."

"April, you are still a child. Maybe someday you'll be able to understand and stop seeing everything from his perspective. You don't know half of what you think you know."

"I'm sorry," she said, sitting next to her mother on the bed. "Will you tell me about it?"

"Not now. But maybe someday when you're ready to hear it, without holding what you remember against me. Go shower. I'll make you a cup of coffee and a snack. Then you can go see him."

"I really am sorry. I just don't know what I'm supposed to do with all this, Mom. I don't know what to do."

With her mother sitting next to her, April wept.

Hair still dripping, she stood outside her bedroom door, feeling nervous about what she might encounter on the other side.

"Here's some coffee," Maye said, appearing behind her.

"I almost don't want to go in. I'm scared to see him."

"It's not that bad, mostly like he's got a bad fever. Don't be scared. Like you said, he needs you."

Coffee in hand, she slowly turned the knob.

The room was dark, with just a hint of the day's light poking through the curtains. Even without the light, she could easily find her way around the room she grew up in. Silently, she moved toward the bed and clicked the reading lamp on to its lowest setting. David stirred in the bed but didn't wake. Looking down at his face, her heart melted. Even in his sleep, he looked plagued by ghosts. His face was fraught, jaws clenched, and his eyelids fluttered wildly. Whatever battle he faced, he looked to be losing. Climbing in the bed, she settled herself next to him, resting her back against the headboard.

She reached down and placed her hand on his forehead. He was cool and clammy. She thought for the millionth time of the night she first met him. About the stunning juxtaposition between the man, the warrior, she met that night, and the man who lay beside her, who was seemingly so weak. *No*, she thought. *He's not weak. He's the strongest person I've ever met, even in this moment of weakness.*

He rolled into her. Resting his head in her lap and let out a deep sigh. As she shifted to get comfortable under his weight, his grip around her tightened, like he was clinging to her in desperation. In that moment, she realized she could never love anybody more than she loved him right now. Her heart welled. Overcome with emotion, she felt tears form in her eyes and begin to trace their way down her face.

She thought about how frail he looked. So small even though he was so great in size. "Oh God, bring your armies down to fight this battle with him. Send every angel you have to him now, when he needs you. You made this man to do what he does, but he needs help, and I am not enough. Father, save him from this misery. Let me take this from him. Let me help carry this burden."

With her words still echoing in the dark room, she felt a fog settle in her mind. Out of the fog, she saw a beautiful smiling blonde woman. She was young, probably around April's age, if not younger. As the woman danced through the fog, David stepped out of it smiling. The blonde called to him to dance, but he shook his head laughing. Suddenly, more and more people began to emerge. All of them walking toward David and the dancing woman.

Their faces were full of joy as they gathered around him, shaking his hand and blessing him. Then she saw a familiar face. Bee stood back, waiting for the line to dissipate. When it had, she walked slowly toward him. Recognizing Bee immediately, David embraced her firmly, nearly lifting her off the ground. As Bee moved away smiling, another form appeared. This one's head was dropped in embarrassment. David walked to the man and lifted his head up. It was Stephen.

"Jesus died for you," David said, his words booming through the endless fog. "My brother, rejoice. The victory has been won. In Jesus name, you are free."

"But," Stephen stammered. "You are fighting this, all on your own."

"Do I look alone?" David answered, sweeping his arm around. "Look around you, Stephen. These are God's beloved children. They are with me."

The dancing woman skipped to David and whispered in his ear, pointing toward April. He laughed heartily at whatever she said and raised his eyes, meeting April's.

"April," he called to her. "I've been looking for you. Come, join the fun."

April felt herself moving through the fog toward his outstretched arms. As she neared, the blonde stopped her. Giving April a quick peck on the cheek, she motioned to all the people gathered. "See how he loves?" she asked. "He says this is an obligation, that he does it for me, but the truth is, God gave him an amazing gift of love. The taking part is just a small part of something much bigger. Don't fear for him, April. He's not alone in this. All of these people pray for him. With them, you, and God on his side, he can't lose."

"It feels so hopeless," April said.

"These things usually do," the blonde answered somberly. "Don't give up on him. It won't be easy, but he is so strong. Be strong for him too. He's waiting for you."

As April began to walk toward him, David and the group dissolved into the fog.

She stayed with him until her feet went numb, praying over him each time he stirred or grumbled in his sleep. Whatever nightmare he faced seemed lessened by her presence. Each prayer quieted him and brought an unusual sense of calm over her. It was odd to her that talking to God calmed her so completely. Just days before, her prayers had felt like a weird ritual, unconnected and almost mandatory, but now in the dark room, it was more like talking to a long-lost friend. So, she prayed.

She prayed for David and this current situation. She prayed for whatever future they might have together. For restoration between herself and her mother, and most importantly, she thanked God for the blessing that the past week had brought. Since she was a young girl she never thought, never imagined, there was any chance of love for her. She hadn't really believed in love. Lust and comfort yes, but love? Love was a Hollywood idea that seemed improbable, and for so long, she had taken her parent's failed marriage as proof of that.

Here in the dark, all of that changed. With his heart beating against her legs and his arms wrapped tightly around her, she realized that she was completely and unequivocally in love with this man. Not in the romantic comedy sort of way, but at her very core, she was yoked to him. How that was possible in one small week, she didn't know. What she did know is that she would spend the rest of her life sharing any burden he felt, taking on any pain that inflicted him, and praying down the warriors of heaven to surround him in anything he did. So, she stayed, until her legs were numb and her heart was full.

As she slowly moved out of his grip, his eyes fluttered open. "April?"

"I'm here, David."

His eyes looked to her, pleading. Then closed again as he fell back into his restless dreams.

She had to force herself to leave his side, but she knew she would need to eat something and move around to stretch her body, especially if she would be with him the rest of the night. The trip down the stairs was a precarious one. Her feet didn't seem to be connected to her any more. She thought about calling out for help but was embarrassed at the absurdity of the situation. Each step felt like the edge of a cliff, so she moved slowly and deliberately, ensuring that one foot was firmly planted in the middle of the step, even if she couldn't feel it, before continuing.

About halfway down, feeling started to return in sharp bursts. Letting out a squeal, she sat down quickly on the step and began to rub her legs.

"April?" she heard from the kitchen.

"Yeah, it's me."

When she rounded the hall to the stairs, Maye burst out laughing. "What on earth are you doing?"

"My legs fell asleep," April answered sheepishly. "I thought I could make it down. I was wrong."

Maye climbed the stairs, meeting her in the middle. "You could have called for me," she said, sitting one step below.

"I know. I just, it just felt silly."

Maye shook her head smiling.

The two sat in silence for a moment before April finally asked, "Mom, will you tell me? You were right. I always took Dad's side. I was so angry at you. I never thought to understand yours."

"You had every right to be. I was not the best mother to you. I tried, really, I did. I could just never get past myself."

"What do you mean?"

"I don't know how to explain it. It seems so trivial now, looking back."

"Will you try?"

"Well, your dad was a popular kid. He was so smart and so handsome. I don't think we were ever really meant to be together."

"That's crazy. I've seen pictures. You were beautiful then, and you're beautiful now."

This time, Maye blushed. "You have to say that, you look like me. Truthfully, if I hadn't gotten pregnant, I don't think we would have ended up together. He was so responsible and focused. He had big dreams, whereas I was the complete opposite. I was and have always been more of a free spirit, never thinking past today.

We never really dated either. Your dad and I just sort of happened. After some harvest party, I think. He, being Mr. Responsible, insisted that we marry. Not that I minded, I was smitten, but he didn't want to marry me. He felt obligated to.

Somewhere along the way, I started to realize that if it weren't for my pregnancy, for you, we would have ended that night. He probably never would have even thought about me again. That tore at me. I always thought he was stuck with me, and I hated myself as much as I loved him. It started with booze, I think you were six or seven. We ran into an old lady friend of his from high school. She still looked amazing. Had two kids and her husband had been killed in the line of duty. He was a cop or a fireman, I can't remember which. In any case, she practically threw herself on your dad. He still had his hair back then.

It killed me to see the type of woman he could have, and I realized I wasn't enough. He tried to tell me otherwise, but this little voice in the back of my mind constantly reminded me, so I drank. It silenced that voice, any voice really, and made me feel prettier, flirtier, more desirable. I think your dad liked it at first, but at some point, that same little voice told me to make him jealous. So, I acted out, like a fool, but I got attention. Soon, that attention became an addiction all its own. I went out of my way to get it. If not from him, then from anybody willing to give it. I never cheated on him, I swear, but it wasn't right the way I acted.

April nodded, remembering her own experiences with the need for male attention, and the lengths she would go to to get it.

"At some point, I think your father gave up. Not that I blame him. I would have done the same if the situation was reversed. Instead of trying to fix it, like an adult, I tried to mask the pain of rejection."

"The pills?"

"You got it. There's a pill for everything nowadays. The more I partied, the further he withdrew. The crazy thing, April, is that all I wanted all those years was for him to want me. The more I tried to be what I thought he wanted, the more I pushed him away."

"Did he ever try to help?"

"He did everything people think they're supposed to do. He offered rehab, changed shifts, wanted counseling, all of that. Not once did he just hold me and tell me he loved me. I think if he would have just reached out to me on that level, things would be so much different now."

"I'm so sorry. I never knew."

"Nor should you have. He wasn't a bad man, April, but he could be a cold man. I'm sorry I let that get to me. I'm truly sorry that I wasn't better for you. Maybe we have a chance now. So, April, let me give you a piece of advice." She looked up toward the bedroom where David slept. "Let yourself be loved."

When the sun had set, leaving behind only traces of its light reflecting brilliantly off clouds in the sky, and the first of the evening stars began to sparkle, April settled into the couch feeling desperate to read more of God's Word. The part of her that felt empty days before was starting to fill with new understanding. Where she once needed to use to fill that space, a new hunger for truth was beginning to gnaw at her spirit. After sitting with David again, she needed God's presence to calm her.

With the Bible open on her lap, she began to pray for guidance. The person she was before she had been for so long, and she needed a new identity. David had provided a foundation for that identity, but with him out of commission, she had started to feel lost again. She knew she had to be strong for him, and she would need to feel strong in herself to get there. She longed to be something more but didn't know where to start. "Show me, Lord." She prayed. "Teach me how to move forward. I'm so afraid to go backwards, and I need your hand to guide me." She flipped through the pages, landing in 1 Peter 5, she began to read:

> To the elders among you, I appeal as a fellow elder and a witness of Christ's sufferings who also will share in the glory to be revealed. Be shepherds of God's flock that is under your care, watching over them—not because you must, but because you are willing, as God wants you to be; not pursuing dishonest gain, but eager to serve; not lording it over those entrusted to you, but

being examples to the flock. And when the Chief Shepherd appears, you will receive the crown of glory that will never fade away. In the same way, you who are younger, submit yourselves to your elders. All of you, clothe yourselves with humility toward one another, because, "God opposes the proud but shows favor to the humble. Humble yourselves, therefore, under God's mighty hand, that he may lift you up in due time. Cast all your anxiety on him because he cares for you. Be alert and of sober mind. Your enemy the devil prowls around like a roaring lion looking for someone to devour. Resist him, standing firm in the faith, because you know that the family of believers throughout the world is undergoing the same kind of sufferings. And the God of all grace, who called you to his eternal glory in Christ, after you have suffered a little while, will himself restore you and make you strong, firm and steadfast. To him be the power for ever and ever.

Amen.

After reading the verses silently on the page, she felt compelled to read them again out loud. As she did, a picture formed in her mind. She saw herself in a car, next to David, driving through open countryside, music playing on the radio. Finally, they stopped in front of a large beautiful church. Once inside, she walked directly to the stage and began to tell her story. She watched as the churchgoers applauded and then saw, near the back, a young woman with tears in her eyes and longing in her soul. April leaped off the stage and walked down the aisle to the girl, to the apparent surprise of the others in attendance. She began to pray over the girl, feeling a sudden heat in her heart. She heard the thundering of drums as victory was won.

The vision faded, and April made a vow to God to spend the rest of her life finding the lost. "A Shepherd," she said out loud, overcome with awe. "Just like in the verse."

As she said amen, she heard an unexpected noise coming from David's backpack. It took her a few minutes to realize that it was his cell phone vibrating. At first, she planned to let it go to voicemail, but some instinct told her to answer.

"Brother, where are you?" a voice asked.

"Uh, he's asleep. Who is this?"

"April?"

"Yes, how'd you know?"

"Oh, hi! This is Caleb, that was probably weird, huh? You're the only person David has mentioned this past week, so I just assumed."

She was immediately drawn to his voice, so full of cheer and life, and she understood why David had opened up to him so many years ago.

"You still there?"

"Oh yeah, sorry. I was thinking. I feel like I know you. David has told me so much."

"All lies I'm sure." Caleb laughed. His voice turning somber, he asked, "Is he okay? I had a feeling that he needed me."

"I'm not sure yet. He…" She paused, unsure of how much to divulge. Deciding David would want him to know everything, she continued. "You know about Stephen, I'm sure." The line was silent. "Caleb?"

He sighed heavily. "Stephen Foster?"

"Yes."

"Yes, I know."

"Well, he, um, we found him, and David took something from him."

"Do you know what?"

"No, but he's not doing well. I found him early this morning in a national forest park. He was covered in mud and half frozen. We got him cleaned up and in bed where he's been since."

"Has he said anything?"

"Incoherent mumbling mostly. He said my name a few hours ago, but that's it."

"April, did he tell you how it works?"

"You mean how he actually takes it on?"

"That's what I mean. What you have to understand is that he takes all of that thing. If there's anything left in the person, then it can grow again, think of it like a weed. To kill the weed, you must kill the root, or it will just come back. That means he takes the parts that made it what it was to begin with. I'm not saying that people don't remember that part, as I'm sure you're aware. They do. It just loses its power over them. That means that he puts those chains on. I read the articles, and Stephen had some serious chains."

April nodded in agreement. "He did."

"This is a unique situation, since David has been in his own prison since Hope died. So now, he's coming to terms with his own cage, while also suffering the chains of his sister's attacker."

"Wait, you know about his prison?"

"Of course. I've known since he left. I don't know how I know, I just somehow saw it, despite that fact that he's hidden it from himself all these years."

"Caleb, I have to tell you. I've had dreams about this."

"Tell me everything."

April started at the beginning. She told about seeing the man in the bar and how later David had seen him in the park. How she had dreamt of the two men in a play-like enactment, Stephen covered in chains and David in his own glass coffin. She told how they had made a plan to find Stephen, and how at first, they had failed. She talked about the night at Phil's when David had turned from her and walked away in the dark. How she had found him and how he tossed and turned in his sleep. When she was finished, she could practically hear Caleb thinking on the other end of the line.

"April," he said at last. "You love him, right?"

"With everything I am."

"Okay, I don't want you to take this the wrong way, but he needs more than that right now. Can you speak out against his enemy?"

"What do you mean?"

"I mean, this is not just a battle. It's a war. He needs God's truth spoken out over him. Can you do that?"

"I...I don't know. Do you mean like an exorcism?"

"Well, kind of, but not really. He's not possessed, he's oppressed. Think of it like getting caught in a wave. Only in this case, it's like hurricane waves, pounding against him and knocking him under, then keeping him down. It's not in him, so to speak, but it's pushing him down, holding him back. Each emotion and memory of what he's taken is like a new wave, and I'm thinking there are a lot. He can tread water, but I think this time he's going to need a little extra help."

"I can try," she answered honestly. "I owe him everything."

"I do too, April, so I'd like to help. I'll book the red eye, tell me your address and I'll text my flight details as soon as I book. For now, just keep loving him."

The call disconnected.

She had planned to sleep on the couch to avoid any sort of impropriety, but her heart ached at the thought of him alone in the dark room. Grabbing her Bible, she climbed the stairs, preparing her heart for battle.

She was again overcome with an irrational fear once outside the door. An unusual panic settled deep in her chest. Logically, she understood that he wasn't possessed, but years of horror movies were clouding her ability to believe what Caleb had told her about the oppression, rather than possession. Those same movies taught her there's nothing worse than an enemy you can't see. *This is ridiculous,* she thought, sliding her back down the closed door, until she was seated on the carpet in front of it. With the Bible on the floor beside her, she decided to search, using the app on her phone, for verses related to victory. If this truly was a battle, fear was holding her back, and she needed ammo to fight it.

The first verses displayed proved to be exactly what she needed, so she prayed them out loud until the fear subsided, replaced with hope.

"No, in all these things, we are more than conquerors through him who loved us. For I am convinced that neither death nor life, neither angels nor demons, neither the present nor the future, nor any powers, neither height nor depth, nor anything else in all creation will be able to separate us from the love of God that is in Christ Jesus our Lord."

With her heart and mind finally at peace, she opened the door.

The light from the hallway washed over the room, falling on the bed where David lay entangled in sheets. His face was still firm, his jaws clenched, and forehead damp. She worked slowly to carefully untangle him from the nest of sheets, twisting and turning his limbs until they were finally free.

Once he was freed, she climbed in next to him, her head once again resting on the headboard, and put one hand on his arm. "I'm here," she whispered. "I'm with you, don't be afraid. You're not alone."

She opened her Bible to the book of Psalm and began reading out loud the words that had comforted him so many times before. At some point, her weariness got the best of her, and her head fell to her chest in a restless sleep.

DAY 8

It felt like she had just closed her eyes when the vibrating of David's phone brought her out of her dreamless nap. David was wrapped around her, so she moved her arm slowly to avoid disturbing him. A text from Caleb.

"Just landed. Be there in twenty."

The clock showed two twenty.

She slipped from David's grasp and left the room, leaving a crack in the door so that he wouldn't be left in the dark. As she descended the stairs, she heard him cry out in agony—the cry of a lost child—and fought the urge to run back to him. "No," she told herself. "You cannot do this alone. You have to be prepared before you can try to save him."

In the kitchen, she started a pot of coffee. While it brewed, her fingers drummed restlessly against the counter. She wasn't sure what to expect from Caleb's visit, but she was hopeful. Just as the pot finished brewing, another text came through.

"Here."

Walking toward the door, she wished she would have thought to freshen up. She hadn't looked at herself since her shower yesterday and could only imagine what sort of death she must look like. Too late now. She opened the door and nearly let out a burst of laughter when she saw the man on the other side. He was nothing like she had imagined. In fact, he was almost the exact opposite. She had pictured another version of David, but this man was at least a full six inches shorter, with a mop of thick blonde hair that nearly reached his shoulders and had not an ounce of meat on his bones. As if reading her mind, he began to chuckle. The same joy she had heard in his voice earlier filled his laugh with a musical quality.

"Hard to believe we're best friends, isn't it?"

"I'm so sorry." She giggled. "I was a little caught off guard. Please, come in. I made coffee."

"Great. I could use a cup, or six. Let's chat." He followed her to the kitchen.

Once their coffee was fixed and they were comfortable at the table, his face turned serious. "This isn't going to be easy. We have to get him to the surface."

"How do we do that?" she asked.

"Really, it's about understanding what he's facing, so we can speak out against it. I think I have a solid grasp on the Stephen side, but I need to know what he was going into it with."

"He was angry," she said. "Before we went to find Stephen, he told us he didn't know if he could do it. He didn't even want me there, said he didn't want me to see what he might become."

"So, the same as in the park?"

"I imagine so. I wasn't at the park. I only know what he told me, and it definitely matched what I saw. It almost seemed like more than just anger. It was like bottled up rage ready to blow."

"April, he put that side of himself in a deep dark closet of his heart so many years ago and would never let it out. I think he's dealt with the other parts before—guilt, abuse, and what not—but his own anger has been hidden for so long. I think that's the part we have to expose. I tried to get him to grieve, and maybe he did to some extent, but that spirit of rage and sadness has haunted him since she died."

"I think, though. In fact, I know there was a moment while they were talking. I couldn't hear what they were saying, but I saw his face change. It was like he softened. I can't really explain it."

"I understand, and that's excellent news. It sounds like his anger at Stephen lessened, so now we have to deal with his anger at God."

She was taken aback by his revelation. In all her time with David, she had never expected that he might be angry at the God he served so wholeheartedly. "That doesn't make sense. He's so faithful."

"I think that's the most amazing thing about him. His capacity for love is so much greater than his own self-preservation. He loves God dearly, but you can love someone and still be angry at them."

"Hope told me the same thing, about his capacity for love."

Now was Caleb's turn for surprise, one eyebrow shot up as he asked, "I'm sorry? Hope told you?"

She blushed at the realization of how absurd it sounded, "Uh. Yeah. When I was with him earlier, before you called, I had a, um, well, a vision, I guess. Hope was in it, along with dozens of people who were thanking him. I think they were the people he's taken from." She paused, feeling awkward.

"Go on," Caleb pushed.

"Well, she told me that his true gift was his ability to love and the taking part is a by-product of that love."

Caleb pondered her words carefully before responding, "I think that makes more sense than any way I could have explained it. Leave it to Hope to recognize that. It explains why it started with me too."

"He's something special, not just because of his gifts either."

"Man, you really do love him. I'll be honest, I was concerned when he mentioned you, but now I think you're exactly what he needs. There's a fire in you, April, a beautiful burning flame. You are like a beacon for him. He hasn't let himself be loved since Hope died. Now it seems there's actually a chance for him. Thank the Lord for putting you on his path."

"Well, maybe there's a chance for us," she said. "I mean, who knows how he really feels about all of this. What happens when this part is over, you know?"

"Don't overanalyze it, kid. He's not like that. I could hear it in his voice the morning he called me, after taking from you. I tried to get him home that day, but God knew better than I. Despite how terrible this whole situation is, there is a great potential for healing here. Okay, let's make a game plan."

He tossed and turned in the bed in some suspended form of awareness. He knew when April was beside him and desperately wanted to call out to her. When he did drift into sleep, an onslaught of dreams barraged him. In some, he was locked in a dark closet, hearing an unknown voice screaming on the other side of the door. In others, he was floating on some sort of raft, tossed by waves with the same screams echoing in his mind. He felt, for the first time in his life, like he no longer wanted to live. He couldn't grasp on to a single thought or emotion and felt as though his very spirit was empty.

When she was beside him, he could feel her warmth, both physically and in his heart. The throbbing pain that clamped onto it subsiding to a dull ache, for at least a moment. When she left and he was alone, the realization of emptiness returned. He was somehow completely void of emotion and simultaneously overwhelmed by it. He knew he was missing something—something that he was supposed to know. A life vest to help keep him afloat, but he'd lost the plot. The darkness in the room creeped into his soul, as shadows creep over the landscape with the waning sun. He tried to fight it, reached in his mind for something, but couldn't grasp it and was left in a free fall. At some point, he felt a new presence in the room and heard the cadence of familiar words.

As the words continued, warmth began to grow in the isolate chambers of his mind. He wanted desperately to open his eyes and welcome the reader, but somewhere in his mind, a voice told him there was nobody there. It told him there had never been anyone there, and he would always be alone. An invisible jury pointed skeletal fingers at him, reminding him that it was his fault.

"You could have saved her." Their hollow voices condemned. "Instead you left her to die, so you will suffer alone. Nobody will ever love the monster you are."

The comfort of the familiar words faded back to the darkness, shut out by the closet door. The screaming woman turned her accusation on him. "It's your fault. You killed her, and then what? You free her attacker? Where were you when she was feeling tortured? Not there to save her, that's for sure. Useless." Her screaming faded, and the despair rose again in his chest.

"To you, Lord, I called; to the Lord I cried for Mercy: what is gained if I am silenced, if I go down to the pit? Will the dust praise you? Will it proclaim your faithfulness? Hear, Lord, and be merciful to me. Lord, be my help."

They talked until almost five that morning. April wanted to set to work immediately, but Caleb insisted on prayer and worship time.

"How long?" she asked.

"As long as it takes. We have to be prepared. We have to put on the full armor of God. Flip open your Bible to Ephesians six. Start in verse eight." She read the words as he continued. "Don't think that we're on the outside of this, April. David has been used by God for tremendous good, which means the enemy is going to do everything he can to stand in the way of his healing, including coming after us. Prepare your heart. The scripture says the devil prowls around like a roaring lion, seeking whom he may devour. May, April, not will. Prayer will prepare us."

So, they had spent hours in prayer, longer than April would have liked, although she would never admit it. After Maye left for work, shocked to wake up to another house guest, Caleb sent April to bed. She tried to fight it, but he was unwilling to relent.

"You have to rest. I'll take care of him for a bit. You sleep."

She did. Or at least she tried to.

When her eyes finally closed, a scene unfolded on the back of her eyelids. She found herself watching a sort of *Judge Judy* courtroom drama, only this dark court was ruled by the shadowy figure of death, and David was the accused. Face after unrecognizable face took the stand, all calling him guilty. His eyes were almost lifeless as he sat accepting the onslaught of lies brought forward, as though they were true. Each witness told stories of his failures, blaming him for whatever hardships they faced. Each one insisting he should have done more for them. With each testimony, David's head sunk lower.

In the corner, a jury box was filled with indistinguishable faces. Each body wore a mask displaying its true nature—guilt, shame, regret—and each one hemmed and hawed with the passing testimonies. She watched as the judge declared David guilty of all charges, slamming a boney gavel down. A sharp-nosed bailiff shackled the un-contesting David and directed him to a gloomy hallway. "Guilty!" the jurors cheered.

"No, David. It's not true," she screamed over the cheering, desperately trying to get his attention. "Fight back. Don't give into these liars."

He looked to her without a glimpse of hope in his eyes. A single tear rolled down his cheek, as he mouthed "guilty" and allowed himself to be pulled away into the gloom.

"Anything?" April asked, setting a fresh mug of coffee on the bedside table.

"He came up to the surface, got a breath, but something pulled him back down. I know he could hear me."

"They've labeled him guilty," April said, sitting in one of the two chairs they had brought from the kitchen earlier.

"That's oddly specific and yet somehow completely vague. Care to expand?"

"These dreams, Caleb. They seem so real. It's like I can see what he's going through. It's not good. He's not even fighting." She felt frustration begin to overcome her. "Why isn't he fighting? He has to fight."

"Okay, I still don't know what you're talking about. What happened in the dream?"

"It was like a court, but not like we're used to. More like Tim Burton style, dark and demented, and all these featureless faces testified against him. It was like they couldn't actually find something he did wrong. They just told him he didn't do enough. And he bought it, Caleb. Every line. He couldn't see how ridiculous it was. He just let them take him down this hallway that goes God knows where."

"Featureless faces, huh? Hand me your Bible, please."

She passed the book to him and watched while he flipped through the pages. "John, John, John, I can't remember where it is," he mumbled, "Oh wait, here. John eight. What's this? Uh. Okay, forty-four. Listen to this, uh, it's down here, okay. 'He was a murderer from the beginning, not holding to the truth, for there is no truth in him. When he lies, he speaks his native language, for he is a liar and the father of lies.'" He read the lines again. "This is what he's trapped in. Satan is the father of lies, and this court you saw is a trap. He's made David believe that he's guilty. I'm sure it wasn't that hard. He's blamed himself for Hope's death for so long. We have to rebuke that." He flipped the pages back again, saying, "Here it is, in Isaiah, 'No weapons forged against you will prevail, and you will refute every tongue that accuses you. This is the heritage of the servants of the Lord, and this is their vindication from me,' declares the Lord."

"Yes!" April said. "Amen! Actually, I think I highlighted one in my app the other day. This might be a useful one." Pulling out her phone, she opened the app and found the highlighted verses in Matthew 5. "Blessed are those who are persecuted because of righteousness, for theirs is the kingdom of heaven. Blessed are you when people insult you, persecute you, and falsely say all kinds of evil against you because of me. Rejoice and be glad, because great is your reward in heaven, for in the same way they persecuted the prophets who were before you."

"Good, April. Yes, yes! Blessed are you, brother. Fight against these lies. Fight to find the light of truth in this darkness. You are accused, but you are innocent of these charges. You have loved and fought for every person you have ever known. Be free, brother. Forgive yourself."

He felt them every time they were in the room. Sometimes, there was only one voice, echoing through the emptiness. Other times, a multitude of voices mingling at the edge of his conscious. Whatever closet he had been trapped in, now fell away and he was nowhere. He was somewhat aware of the fact that he was not actually in whatever place this was, but it all felt so real. He could see endless plains of blackness, swirling around like currents, could feel his breath exiting his body, but couldn't identify what the place was.

He tried to move toward the voices, but each step he took sent them in a new direction, neither closer nor further than they had been before. He felt his heart ache to be with them again. He wasn't sure who they were, but he knew that he knew them and cared for them deeply. He longed for them and for something else. A deeper ache stirred in his heart for a familiar light.

"Please," he whispered into the void.

DAY 9

She sat with him, while Caleb took a turn to sleep. She was supposed to be reading to him but spoke to him instead. How was it possible to miss somebody you barely knew this much?

"I'm here," she said, taking his hand between her own. Whatever hell David was trapped in was beginning to impact him physically. Dark circles had formed under his eyes, despite being in an almost constant state of sleep, his face was tight with jaws clenched, and his muscles had started to shake in periodic spasms. "Come back to me now. You've been gone long enough. Come back."

She spoke to him of her childhood, telling him things she never thought she would. She spoke more about her father and what it had been like when he had left, how he didn't even tell her; he was just gone one day. She told how it was two years between the time he left and the time he tried to see her again. "I was so mad, David. How can you do that to someone you claim to love? It should be impossible to leave like that. But he did."

As the hours passed, so did her ability to think of new stories to tell. The afternoon faded to evening, bringing with it an uneasy feeling. Caleb tried to cheer her up, but she felt trapped. She hadn't dreamt anything since the court room dream and felt like she was leaving him all on his own, without any sort of support.

"I just don't know what to do, Caleb," she said when he came in with a plate of sandwiches for them. "How long does this take?"

"I don't know if there's any set timeframe. Don't forget what we talked about yesterday, this isn't just him dealing with what he took, he's dealing with himself too. Most of us take years battling through the experiences of our lives that have us in bondage in the first place. He just kind of skipped that part, so now all of those things are coming back."

"I'm really starting to think we should go with my ice water idea. It always worked when my mom was out."

Caleb laughed, nearly choking on his turkey sandwich. "Yeah, not sure how well that'd work in this situation. Most likely, you'd end up with a soggy bed and have to figure out how to get him out of it, and I'm not helping."

For the first time since she had answered the door for Caleb, April smiled. "You're right, that is not going to happen. I don't even know if the two of us could lift his dead weight." Her smile tightened when she recognized her poor word choice.

"Come on, April, this isn't his end."

"How do you know?" she demanded, standing abruptly to pace. "You said it yourself, who knows how these things go. What happens if he just doesn't wake up? We can't force-feed him."

"It won't come to that."

"How do you know?"

"Faith is the confidence that what we hope for will actually happen. It gives us assurance about the things we cannot see."

She paused, staring at him. "He said that once."

"Well, it's true."

"So we just believe it?"

"We believe it, we pray it, we speak it over him. What did you read while I was asleep?"

She blushed sheepishly. "I kind of didn't. I mean, I started to but then I just talked to him. I need him to know I'm here. I haven't had any more dreams so I feel like I'm not with him anymore, and he has to know I'm with him." She could tell Caleb was slightly annoyed with her but didn't push it. "Where should we pick up?"

"Why don't we leave it up to chance, pull out your app?"

She handed him her phone and watched as he closed his eyes and scrolled over. Finally landing on one, he said, "Well, this is interesting. It's not often one finds themselves in Habakkuk."

"Ha-what?"

"Habakkuk. Yeah, so, listen to this, 'How long, O Lord, must I call for help? But you do not listen. Violence is everywhere! I cry, but you do not come to save. Must I forever see these evil deeds? Why must I watch all this misery? Wherever I look, I see destruction and violence. I am surrounded by people who love to argue and fight. The law has become paralyzed, and there is not justice in the courts. The wicked far outnumber the righteous, so that justice has become perverted.'"

"The judgment, again. What now?"

"Now, I think we need some words from another man who was trapped."

"Who?"

"Jonah."

"Like, with the whale?"

"Technically, it was a fish. But yes, that's the one."

"How will that help?"

He moved his finger across the screen of her phone and handed it to her. "Read this."

She read the words out loud, "Then Jonah prayed to the Lord his God from inside the fish. He said, "I cried out to the Lord in my great trouble, and he answered me. I called to you from the land of the dead, and Lord you hear me! You threw me into the ocean depths, and I sank down to the heart of the sea. The mighty waters engulfed me; I was buried beneath your wild and stormy waves.""

She continued to read until the end of the chapter, finishing with, "But I will offer sacrifices to you with songs of praise, and I will fulfill all my vows. For my salvation comes from the Lord alone."

She was back, talking to the other presence. He knew it was a familiar one, but he couldn't understand who would be here. In the darkness, he heard the words they spoke. Each one falling on him like drops of rain, soaking through his clothes. Each droplet reflected light from the darkness. It was odd to him that light would come from vast nothingness. He began to watch them falling around him with their unreal luminescent quality. He stood to his feet, surrounded now by glowing puddles and moved through the emptiness. As more and more of the word drops fell over him, the puddles began to meet, forming a stream that grew into a wide churning river.

Suddenly, from within the river, a dark form emerged. A giant black dragon walked from the river, shaking the glowing drops from its scales. Its eyes searched for him. Finally landing on him, it let out a mighty roar in his direction. He thought to run but knew there was nowhere to hide in the vastness of this void. The dragon climbed up the newly formed banks hissing "guilty" through curled fangs. It rose up on its hind legs and inhaled a deep breath, preparing to surround him in its flame.

I've seen this before, he thought, fighting in his mind to remember how he knew of this dragon. He felt words begin to fill his heart and pour out from his mouth. "Then I heard a loud voice in heaven say, 'Now have come the salvation and the power and the kingdom of our God, and the authority of his Messiah. For the accuser of our brothers and sisters, who accuses them before our God day and night, has been hurled down. They triumphed over him by the blood of the Lamb, and by the word of their testimony; they did not love their lives so much as to shrink from death. Therefore, rejoice, you heavens and you who dwell in them! But whoa to the earth and sea, because the devil has gone down to you! He is filled with fury, because he knows that his time is short.'"

They both paused, looking up from their Bibles, when David suddenly began to whisper. April stared down at him, her mouth opened in awe, not sure what to expect.

"He's remembering, April. Oh, praise Jesus!"

Mumbled words continued to slide through David's pursed lips. "For the accuser of our brothers and sisters, who accuses them before our God day and night, has been hurled down. They triumphed over him by the blood of the Lamb and by the word of their testimony." He continued.

"What is it?" April asked.

"Revelation twelve, I'm not sure what verses. It's the woman and the dragon. Here, he handed the Bible back to her. "Pull it up. It's an interesting read. Start at the top."

April read over the chapter. "I don't understand. What does it mean?"

"I don't know." Caleb sighed, running his fingers through his hair. "I know it's a good sign. I just don't know what it means. Can we assume that maybe he's facing a dragon? At least, he is seeing truth in the word. Let's go back to Psalm twenty-five. That's practically been his roadmap since he was a kid."

April turned back to Psalm and began reading out loud from the page, "In you Lord, my God, I put my trust…"

The dragon snarled again. This time, through a long hiss, it said, "You failed. She's dead because of you. What sort of man lets his sister, whom he claimed to love, take her own life like that?" The beast began to circle around him, gnashing it's teeth. "For what? For some pathetic man you didn't even know?"

He felt despair begin to fill his heart again with its inky blackness and noticed glimmering shackles appear on his wrists.

"Come without a fight," it hissed. "I'll let you go peacefully. It's more than you deserve. More than Hope got."

"What do you know?" he cried out at the monster. "What do you know?"

"I know you weren't there. You didn't see her. While you were off running some measly task for your God, I was there." The mouth of the creature curled into a hideous grin. "Your God did this, David. He's as guilty as you."

David felt heat forming in his chest, a flame of rage growing until it burst from his mouth in a fiery roar. "No! You are a liar, you are deceit. You took her from us with your slick tongue. You destroyed her. You set your evil upon that poor boy, let it turn him into a monster like you. This is on you. All of it is on you."

The word drops began to fall again. This time lighting up the darkness with all the glory of the sun.

The beast snarled as the light fell on his scales, revealing dust and mold, and the true nature of itself. "What is this?" it asked, the words searing its flesh.

David could hear her. He could see the words as she read them and joined in, saying out loud the words that brought him comfort in so many times of darkness, "My eyes are ever on the Lord, for only he will release my feet from the snare. Turn to me and be gracious to me, for I am lonely and afflicted. Relieve the troubles of my heart and free me from my anguish. Look on my affliction and my distress and take away all of my sins. See how numerous are my enemies and how fiercely they hate me! Guard my life and rescue me. Do not let me be put to shame, for I take refuge in you. May integrity and uprightness protect me, because my hope, Lord, is in you."

The beast dropped down on all four legs again. Screaming in agony, it ran from him, away from the light, back into the blackness of the void.

He felt something change in his spirit. Something was breaking. His long-held guilt for her death. The weight lifted from his shoulders, and the shackles on his wrists fell into a puddle.

In the distance, he saw a dancing figure. She was radiant. She hopped through puddles laughing as she neared him. "Hope?" he asked, not believing his eyes.

"Finally, dear brother. It took you long enough. What's it been? Seven years?"

"How?"

"I've been waiting for you."

"For what?"

"To forgive yourself. It wasn't your fault, David."

"But I should have been there for you."

"You were, David. You are the reason I tried to stop it. I was just too late. After I took the pills, I started to think about you. How strong you are, a rock David, so firm and so true, and I wanted to find that again. In those last few months, I lost sight of who I was and how God saw me. I didn't feel like his daughter, or beloved. I was trapped in a void, like this one, only I was unwilling to let the word of truth in. I felt like, I don't know. Dirty? I could have asked you to take it, but I wasn't sure if the Holy Spirit would allow you to, and I knew that would destroy you, so I prayed for God to keep you away from me. I couldn't let you see me like that, or feel what I was feeling. Then that night, I saw myself in the mirror, but it wasn't me anymore. I saw this demonic-like face looking back at me, and I had to kill it. By that time, I'd already had, well, too much to drink. I was out of it, David. I just remember knowing that I had to kill it. By the time I realized it was me, and I was seeing a reflection of my misery, it was too late. It was a dirty trick. I thought of you though, and I tried to make myself purge it all back up, but it was too late. Don't you see? You did what you could have done for me. It wasn't your fault. Come now."

She led him to the shore of the river. "Come and be baptized."

Praying over him, she dunked him into the glowing river. "Be free, brother."

He exploded up from the bed gasping for air. Looking around the room, he saw them all staring at him, disbelief written on their faces.

"Brother!" Caleb nearly shouted, catching himself mid-word. "Brother," he whispered.

April jumped up from her chair, letting her Bible slide from her lap with a thump. In one bound, she leapt onto the bed, folding herself over him in tears.

"Good Lord, April. Be careful." Maye scolded, with a mischievous grin on her face. "Welcome back, David."

He was overwhelmed with joy, seeing his best friend next to him. He held tightly to April, asking, "When did you get here?"

"Early yesterday morning. You've been out for about three days. Had us worried for a minute."

"What...what happened?" April stammered through sobs.

"I found Hope."

"Here, let's get you cleaned up. You smell terrible." Caleb laughed, tears forming in his eyes.

"Ah yes, always the honest one, aren't you?" David laughed in return.

April clung to him, as though she were scared he might fall into the sleep that consumed him for three days. He had to peel her off himself to make it to the shower. He was someone convinced she might sit outside the door until he was done. Luckily, Maye herded her downstairs to begin prepping a meal.

In the shower, he let the hot water run over his face, deeply inhaling the steam and letting it work to clear his mind and soften his muscles. He thought about Hope again. Only this time, he was filled with tremendous joy and peace. Taking comfort in the life she had, not getting lost in the moments she would never get. The water washed over him, separating him from the past three days.

When he finished, he met the group in the kitchen. They looked at him expectantly, well, all but April. April looked at him with something else—something like worry that he might disappear again. "Blink, April." He laughed. "It's over."

"It's over?" she asked.

"It's over."

Maye served up grilled cheese sandwiches and chips, then took her seat. "Tell us, David. What happened?"

"I don't even know where to begin. I don't know if it's worth rehashing. Most of it was just emptiness."

"Mom," April said, "don't push."

"Actually," Caleb interjected, "I'm with Maye here. Seeing you in there like that, it brought up some pretty interesting questions."

"Don't encourage her." April grimaced. "Do we really have to relive the whole thing? I never want to think about it again."

"Okay, fine." Caleb agreed. "Just one question. What was with the Revelations reference? Do you remember?"

He nodded, smiling. "Yeah, I remember. It was the weirdest dream ever, if you can call it a dream. I was in this black void, nothingness really. Then suddenly, I heard your voice." He looked at April. "There in the void, I could hear you speaking. I didn't know what you were saying, but the words formed these little drops of water, and they grew and grew, finally forming a river. Out of the river climbed a dragon, he wanted to kill me. I remember him getting ready to spit fire at me, and I realized I recognized him, from Revelation. Well, I didn't realize where it was from, but I remembered the words. So, I spoke them. The dragon did not like it. He called me guilty, told me he would take me peacefully. It stopped word raining for a minute, and then I heard you again; only this time, I remembered all of the words from Psalm. When you spoke them, the whole place lit up. It wasn't really a place, so I guess that doesn't make sense, but the nothingness grew immensely bright. There was so much power in those words. It reminded me of my purpose, of the truth. I think that scared the beast off. He ran, then Hope showed up, dancing, her usual self."

"She's so lovely," April said.

David looked at her, eyebrows arched. "Oh? So, you've met her?"

Meeting his gaze, April answered, "She came to me while I was lying next to you. She told me you would be okay and showed me all the people you've helped."

"Well, she told me the truth of her death. Her thoughts in those last minutes. She told me it wasn't my fault, and that she never wanted me to have to take from her. Then she baptized me in the word river."

"In the what?" Maye asked.

"I don't know what else to call it. There wasn't really a logical sequence of events here."

"Okay, so I have to ask another one. What was the rest of it like? I thought I could let it go, but I don't think I can," Caleb said.

"There's not much to describe. Mostly darkness, overwhelming emotion. It wasn't pleasant, that much I can say. I also know"—he reached out, taking April's hand—"I could feel you every time you were near me. When you were there, it almost felt like there was a way out. I remember clinging to the thought of you, even though I didn't really know that you were you. Again, hard to explain."

"Well, that's about enough of that," Maye said. "Past is past. Let it be where it is."

"One more thing." All three heads turned to him. "April, in that darkness, you were the light. Your voice carried God's words to me, on weird luminescent rain. I don't ever want to experience that darkness again. But if I'm called to it, I want to know that you will be there by my side. My beacon, my hope, and my partner. April, marry me?"

Maye's mouth fell open, as she and Caleb turned toward April in anticipation.

"Yes, one thousand times, yes."

EPILOGUE

He gripped her hand tightly as he drove down the highway. Somehow, he had managed to talk her into coming back to Kansas City with him, much to Maye's dismay. That dismay was lightened when she received an invitation to the O'Luain Thanksgiving celebration, just over one short month away.

He couldn't help but smile at her, as she sang along to the radio, the sun's light bringing out the brilliance of her emerald eyes. Her face was practically glowing as they drove through open countryside, the harsh reality of winter hadn't yet reached the eastern plains of Colorado. With the window down, she let her hand fly through the air.

Suddenly, she sat up straight in the seat beside him. "David, we have to stop. Somewhere around here, we have to stop."

"Restroom break?"

"No, not that. There's a church. I'm supposed to be there."

They took the next exit, driving through a small town, finally stopping in front of a large beautiful church.

"What now?" he asked.

"There's someone in there that needs me."

She opened the door and jumped out of the car.

He followed, like he planned on doing for the rest of his life.

ABOUT THE AUTHOR

JHieb spends her time in the country with her two dogs, enjoying the peace and quiet. She enjoys spending time with her family and participating in local church activities. She sees her writing as a part of her ministry and understands that life, even as a Christian, isn't always pretty. She plans to continue writing about those darker sides and what it means to overcome.

CPSIA information can be obtained
at www.ICGtesting.com
Printed in the USA
LVHW111444290721
694053LV00003B/10